THE RIVER RISING
The Effie Afton Affair

by Ted McElhiney

All rights reserved.
Printed in the United States of America.

The paper in this publication meets the minimum requirements
of American National Standard for Information Sciences--
Permanance of Paper for Printed Library Materials.
(alk. paper)

© Copyright 2004 Ted McElhiney

McElhiney, Ted

The River Rising-The Effie Afton Affair
by Ted McElhiney

TMCELHINEY@AOL.COM

FORWARD

This writing, although fiction, has a basis in fact.
Our story involves the Mississippi River, the events that happened during the 1850s, including the murder of Colonel Davenport;
the slave issue; the destruction of the steamer "Effie Afton" and the burning of the bridge;
the river pilots; the trial; and Abe Lincoln, the lawyer defending the bridge.
Some of the characters in the book are the author's own idea of who they were and how certain historical events might have evolved through their story.

ACKNOWLEDGEMENTS:

An account of the Effie Afton Case
By Marquis Childs from a book,
"Mighty Mississippi Biography Of A River"

The Effie Afton Case
By Carl Sandberg
"Abraham Lincoln-The Prairie Years"

"Banditti of the Prairie"
By Edward Bonney

"Steamer Effie Afton vs. The Rock Island Bridge"
By Greg Pelo

"Lincoln: Prairie Lawyer"
By John J. Duff

"The Real Lincoln"
By Jesse William Weik

*For Jan...who continues to stand by...
with constructive criticism*

PREFACE

The valley of the Mississippi River from its earliest settlement has been more infested with reckless and bloodstained men than any other part of the country, being more congenial to their habits and offering the greatest inducements to follow their nefarious and dangerous trades.
Situated as it is, of great commercial importance, and the river whose name it bears, together with its tributaries stretching four thousand miles north from the Gulf of Mexico, and draining all the country south and west of the great chain of lakes, between the Allegheny and the Rocky Mountains, it has afforded them an unequaled chance to escape detection and pursuit, and thus wooed as it were, countless villains and bloodstained, law-doomed ones to screen themselves in its bosom.

Organized bands, trampling upon right, and defying all law human or divine, have so annoyed the peaceful and quiet citizens of this great valley, that in the absence of a sufficient judicial power the aid of "Judge Lynch" has been but too frequently called in. And a neighboring tree proved a gallows and "a short shrift and strong cord" have been the doom of those who have ever plead vainly for mercy at his bar.
But this mode of summary punishment only served to drive those really guilty from one section of the country to another, changing for a time their plan of action and

operations without, in the least, reforming or exterminating them, while in many instances the innocent were made to atone for the crimes of the guilty.

It would be useless to attempt to enumerate the thousand robberies and scores of murders committed from time to time by the organized and lawless united Banditti. Our task shall be simply and plainly to detail the particulars of a few of the many committed by that portion of the gang infesting the country bordering on the Upper Mississippi.
It was chosen to show how the murder of Colonel George Davenport at Rock Island was instigated by many different factions existing at that time along the River, and how certain political causes might have influenced high ranking politicians to seek out the Banditti to perform the murderous deeds to suit their wants.
Nauvoo, Illinois, the headquarters of the Mormon chief and his satellites, had already increased to a population of eighteen thousand. Many of the Banditti offenders were frequently tracked in the direction of Nauvoo, where the accused were immediately released by the city authorities on the grounds that the complaint was *"Persecution against the Saints,"* effectively drowning the pleas for justice of the injured. The arresting officer thus forced to return and tell the tale of defeat. This done, the fugitives found a safe shelter under the wide-spread wings of the Mormon leaders. Many of these perpetrators worked their way up the Mississippi River to Rock Island, Illinois, doing daring robberies and other atrocities with all roads leading back to Nauvoo connections.

Governor Ford was aware of the conditions and dispatched troops to subdue and preserve order in the vicinity around the Mormon stronghold.

All being tranquil, Ford thinking all was well, he disbanded his troops.

Soon, however, complaints from the surrounding country told that the ruffians were again at work, and as heretofore, all attempts to bring the offenders to justice proved abortive.

If arrested, witnesses were always ready to swear them clear, and all again were in a state of disorder and fear.

The smouldering fires were again ready to burst forth, and riot and bloodshed take the place of law and order. Another tragedy was to be enacted, fearful and bloody, and another victim sent unprepared into the presence of his Maker.

*Above excerpts are taken from Edward Bonney's book
"The Banditti of the Prairies-
A Tale of the Mississippi Valley."*

CONTENTS

CHAPTER 1:
A COLONEL ELIMINATED

CHAPTER 2:
WAITING IT OUT AT ROCK ISLAND

CHAPTER 3:
THE ATTEMPT TO STOP THE ROCK ISLAND BRIDGE

CHAPTER 4:
AN ATTEMPT TO BURN THE BRIDGE BY BOATMEN

CHAPTER 5:
TAKING ON A RAPIDS PILOT

CHAPTER 6:
THE WEATHER APPEARS TO BE LETTING UP

CHAPTER 7:
THE EFFIE AFTON HITS THE BRIDGE AND BURNS

CHAPTER 8:
A CLUE FOUND ON THE WRECKAGE

CHAPTER 9:
SABOTAGE OR ACCIDENT

CHAPTER 10:
GETTING ACQUAINTED IN LECLAIRE

CHAPTER 11:
SHOOTING THE RAPIDS

CHAPTER 12:
THE WRIT HAS BEEN FILED

CHAPTER 13:
THE SPRINGFIELD LAWYER APPEARS AT THE BRIDGE

CHAPTER 14:
THE TRIAL BEGINS IN CHICAGO

CHAPTER 15:
LINCOLN STATES HIS CASE

Remembering

*Millions of mornings
the Mississippi awakes
and rolls
over fish, stones,
and old dead bones.
In the early morning
the sun lays back
of the horizon.
Animals meet the call
of the old river
as best they can.
In the evening
the forgotten tones
of the mark call hang
above the water.
She remembers the rapids
of her upper waters
and Captains courageous.*

Poem by
Max J. Molleston
Davenport, Iowa

1

CHAPTER ONE:
A COLONEL
ELIMINATED

The big majestic stone home of Colonel Davenport was built on the Illinois bank of the Mississippi River, facing the Iowa shore. It served as a fort and trading post for residents and traders dealing with the Indians.

The Colonel stood on the porch of his home, insisting that the members of his family go without him to the celebration that was planned for that hot July day at the Rock Island courthouse. It was the Fourth of July, 1845. The Colonel was tired because of a rough week of debates over the planned location of the railroad bridge. He hoped the issue would soon be settled. This new railroad bridge, if approved for Rock Island, would soon span the Mississippi River and be the tie to the new western sections of the United States. The argument the Colonel had made over and over to the government officials was that the location here at Rock Island would better serve the entire nation because of its proximity to Chicago. Chicago was already becoming a highly industrialized city with a thriving railroad center.

The Colonel waved to the last of his family, who were heading for the celebration of the American Independence being held at the Rock Island courthouse.
He hated missing such a wonderful event with his family, but thought his time better spent reviewing his thoughts and notes concerning the bridge problem. He needed to work on some of his new ideas which he would submit to officials, and to write letters to some of his Washington friends whom he felt he could count on for backing him when the decision of bridge placement came up for finalization. The family would enjoy the celebration, and that was very important to him. He could celebrate later. Hopefully, at the site of the new bridge.

The Colonel turned and went into the house, heading for his parlor. He settled down in his favorite chair, lit his pipe and began to read the newspaper, with an occasional glance up to see the turbulent motion of the Mississippi River as it rushed by his lovely home.
His attention was suddenly interrupted when he heard a

faint noise outside.

"Must be some children playing out by the well or it's just someone drawing water," he thought.

Returning to his reading again, another noise startled him. Thinking he'd better go check it out, he rose from his chair, and headed toward the door to see what was causing the commotion. As he stepped to the door, he saw a shadowy figure cross in front of the door and he knew by its size it was an adult, and not a child.

"What do you want?" he shouted.

The shadowy figure suddenly filled the doorway. It was no one that the Colonel could immediately identify because the intruder was silhouetted against the blinding sunlight from outside.

Suddenly the door pushed open and three men stood before him. Still no one he could recognize. Nothing extremely unusual, as many people wanting something from the trading center often came to the house.

Three men bolted into the room, shoving him violently. Not a word was said. One discharged his pistol at the Colonel, hitting him in the left thigh. The Colonel fell backward in pain as he tried to reach for his cane. Feeling the hot sticky substance coming from his leg, he knew he was bleeding profusely. He tried to right himself to a position in which he could protect himself. His left side was painful and unstable.

The bullet was lodged in his upper left leg and he was unable to stand. One of the intruders looked familiar, but the Colonel was in too much pain to remember who this intruder might be. At first glance something in his mind flashed-- "something about the bridge."

"Could this be someone with a grudge concerning the bridge? Yes," he surmised as he wrenched in pain.

Thoughts of having survived Indian warfare, the dangers of the Mexican war, and the lonely residence here on the very outskirts of civilization sent visions through his throbbing brain. How could this be happening to him when everything seemed so right and so peaceful now?

After thirty years at this place, he, in the last couple of years, had never felt so secure.
But now! Everything in a moment had gone crazy!

The three men rushed upon him, blindfolded him, tied his arms and legs and dragged him by his long gray hair into the hall and up the stairs to a closet, containing an iron safe. The leader demanded money as they were unable to open the safe themselves. Barely alive, the Colonel unlatched the private bolt. They took out the contents and then dragged him into another room and placed him on a bed. With terrible threats, they demanded more money. The old man pointed his feeble hand to a nearby dressing table drawer. He hoped this would satisfy them and they would leave and be gone. The intruders missed the drawer containing the money, opened another, found nothing and became enraged, thinking their defenseless victim had deceived them.

They flew upon him, beating and choking him until he passed out. Next they tried to revive him by dashing him with water. When he came around they again demanded money. Following his pointing hand they again missed the drawer which he indicated. Fiendish brutality pursued until the Colonel again fainted. They doused him, beat him into oblivion, and then threatened "to fry him upon coals of fire." Eventually, the invaders found a few hundred dollars in cash, a gold watch, a shotgun and a pistol. They left the house with blood splattered from parlor to chamber, and with the vulnerable old pioneer bleeding profusely upon the bed.

The Colonel was dead.

Early May 1856, Captain James Brickle, (officer in charge of the J.B. Carson,) on board the riverboat, sat at the Rock Island levee waiting to be one of the first steamboats to pass through the new railroad bridge. Brickle recalled hearing the hideous story of the murderous deed causing the death of Colonel Davenport. He learned the facts from friends and members of the Davenport family he had known. They had told him their version of the terrible murder.

The Colonel had been admired and respected not only because of his valor as a soldier in the Mexican War, and his tireless efforts in establishing a new frontier, but also for his persistent determination to see a railroad bridge located and built here at Rock Island, becoming the entrance to another new frontier. It was something he felt and knew was "right." Many thought he was murdered because of his determination and influence to get the bridge placed in Rock Island.

It seemed there were really five men involved in the Colonel's murder. Four had been captured and identified as the Colonel's murderers: later named as Judge Fox, Birch, John Long and Aron Long. All were harbored at Nauvoo, Illinois and Montrose, Iowa. They were known to be members of the so called "Banditti's of the Prairie," robbing, killing and pillaging up and down the Mississippi River Valley. It was later proven they had strong ties with groups from Saint Louis. Many felt the Colonel was murdered, not for the six hundred dollars they stole, but because of his influence concerning the acquisition for getting the bridge built at the place almost adjacent to his trading post at Rock Island. This was not popular with certain factions in Saint Louis.

Brickle heard the story about how the four men were apprehended. It seemed that a lawman by the name of Ed Bonney infiltrated the band of "Bandittis". Using every trick Bonney knew, he chased the gang from Illinois, through Missouri, over to Ohio, catching them one at a time. Finally, he gained enough information and evidence to have three of them convicted and eventually hanged for their crimes. Still, two had been able to escape capture.

The bridge was built.

"Now, here we are waiting to go up through that very controversial bridge," Brickle lamented as he relit his pipe.

2

CHAPTER TWO: WAITING IT OUT AT ROCK ISLAND

Two weeks earlier, spring had begun to peek, a tint of green was showing through the brown hillsides, and migrating waterfowl had determined it was time to head back up north. "V" formations were appearing everywhere against the gray sky. An occasional pop-pop could be heard as hunters were busy adding to their food supplies. The cold, damp weather this time of the year wasn't to Brickle's liking. He came from a milder part of the country. Missouri! The northwest wind blowing as it was would give a man a chill right down to the bone.

"Won't get any better either once we get past this bridge and are headed north to Saint Paul," he thought.

May 4, 1856...the Steamboat Effie Afton, its Captain and part owner, J.S. Hurd, reached the docks at Rock Island, Illinois, on a maiden voyage up the Mississippi River, bound for Saint Paul. Veteran pilot, Captain James Parker was at the wheel. The Afton was a brand new boat with a large cargo of freight, passengers and livestock.

She was a finely finished boat from stem to stern. The interior decor was in the luxurious "Lake-boat" style. Two hundred and forty feet long, and thirty-five feet wide, drawing five feet of water. The cost to build her was $45,000. On this, her maiden voyage, were sixty passengers in the upper cabins with another one-hundred plus on the next lower deck. Many of the lower deck passengers were from Warren County in Missouri, and several others were from Germany on their way to Minnesota, hoping to establish new homes and a new beginning . The cargo on the main deck consisted mainly of machinery, perishable items, wholesale, and grocery goods, a dozen oxen, nine cows with calves, one colt, four wagons, several cooking stoves, hardware and some personal belongings that would be needed in the great Northwest. This cargo nearly filled every foot of space on board. Most of it was loaded on the first deck by the Germans themselves.
They were all waiting, as the Effie Afton was, for the wind to subside.

Several other boats, docked along with the J.B. Carson and the Effie Afton, were the Tishomingo, the Kate Paulding, the Hamburg, the Clara Dean, the MattieWayne, and the Ben Bolt. All lay at Rock Island, waiting as the Effie Afton was forced to do, the wind giving no indication that it would calm down so they could get underway. Each wanted to be the first to go through the new bridge. The wind had been blowing hard for two days from the northeast, making it impossible to run the bridge.

Boat steerage would be impossible. The profile of the boats would be like putting up a sail for the wind to catch and the power of the wind would send the boat in a direction not desired. The helmsman would have little or no control over his boat. It had been blowing like this for better than two days.

A day earlier, two boats, impatient with waiting, had attempted to make the passage and had failed, finding the challenge to be too much for the risk involved.

The channel of the river at Rock Island, was very swift (high, rising and turbulent), because of the early, wet spring weather. The churning river ran along the northwestern side of the island. Looking up river from the pilot house of the J.B. Carson, one could see, in the hazy distance, the form of a gray, ghostly structure which spanned from Illinois to Iowa, acting as a gateway into the most treacherous rapids on the Mississippi River. Entering this portion of the river required an experienced pilot. Most of the sought-after pilots had been acquired or contracted at LeClaire, Iowa.

Squinting, you could make out six massive stone piers supporting the imposing structure, three within the Iowa boundary and three on the Illinois side. They were engineered and built to support the large wooden superstructure. In the middle of the span was a great pier on which swung a 386 foot revolving section. It swung one hundred and eighty degrees when opened. It made room for the riverboats to pass easily through the bridge. This great bridge contained over 400,000 pounds of wrought iron and 290,000 pounds of cast iron. The superstructure was constructed from over 1,080,000 board feet of lumber, making it the largest drawspan bridge in the United States. The drawspan was necessary to accommodate the steamboats with their tall, scrollworked smokestacks, thus allowing them to pass through the opened section of the bridge without any structure changes to the boats.

Originally, the suggestion to build a suspension bridge, having no piers for steamboats to ram, seemed to be a more practical and a better solution. However, how high would it have to be? The steamboat owners would take great pains to make their stacks as tall as necessary to defeat the design-- hence, a revolving center swinging drawspan was chosen to accommodate the large steamboats.

Great as it was, the bridge had its enemies...!

CHAPTER THREE:
THE ATTEMPT TO STOP THE ROCK ISLAND BRIDGE

Captain Brickle was deep in thought, reminiscing about what had gone on during the controversy over who would get the bridge. He remembered some of the efforts by those who especially didn't want it placed at Rock Island. They had gone to great lengths to keep it from happening.

Even Murder!

Such a dastardly deed was deep within "southern reasoning" if it would stop the bridge being built at Rock Island.

"Kill anyone whose influence could make it happen" was the cry up and down the river, Brickle recalled.

The one person who had stood in the way of the southern concept was the highly decorated, retired veteran of the "Mexican War", Colonel Davenport. Colonel Davenport resided and was murdered in Rock Island, and his name was identified with much influence concerning the bridge conception, its planning, and its placement.

Colonel Davenport was universally loved and esteemed for his generous heart and social qualities, both at home and among his acquaintances in Washington. His wealth had been acquired as an Indian trader. He was an Englishman by birth, but had come to America at an early age. One of the first and true pioneers of the march of civilization into the great Northwest, his hold upon the affections of the residents of that part of the territory was strong. And his abiding messages were passed on to the great leaders of the country, many thinking his influence helped locate the bridge in Rock Island.

The Colonel was murdered, but the bridge was built at his choice of places- Rock Island, adjoining his trading post.

Another question which had had a decisive bearing on where the bridge was to be placed was the question of western extension of slavery. The year in which Florida was purchased, the question arose as to whether slavery should be permitted to establish itself beyond the Mississippi, in the northern part of the territory of Louisiana, then called the Missouri territory. Congress had shut out slavery in 1787 from the Northwest Territory, and dialogue began as to whether slavery should, in like manner, be shut out from that part of the country beyond the Mississippi, north of a line drawn west from the point where the Ohio River joins at the Mississippi River. Fear loomed that trouble would brew between the states.

The reason for this fear was that a great change had come over the country. Before, and even during the revolution, every colony held Negroes in bondage. But in the North, the slaves were chiefly house-servants, and their numbers were never very large. In the South, however, the planters raised all their crops by slave labor, and the numbers of Negro slaves were constantly on the increase. In the North, a bad feeling developed towards slave ownership and there were laws passed which gave slaves their freedom.

This was not the case in the South, because the planters did not see how they could free their slaves without ruining their businesses. On the whole, the effect of the slave system seemed destined now to divide the nation. The people of the two sections not only thought differently about the right and wrong of holding Negroes in bondage, but their business interests had come to be different, The South devoted all its strength to raising cotton, rice and tobacco. Whatever manufactured goods it needed , it had to buy -- such as cloth, shoes, and hats. As Europe could make such goods much cheaper than the United States possibly could, the South naturally wished for free trade, in order that it might import its supplies from the other side of the Atlantic. The North, on the other hand, had gradually come to devote much of its labor and its money to making cloth and other goods. For this reason, the North was opposed to free trade in these articles. It wished to tax European imports and keep foreign goods high, Thus inducing people to buy U.S. products instead. Naturally, while the South wanted liberty to send abroad for goods, the North believed that the country would be better served if manufacturers were protected and encouraged by the government to make those manufactured goods in the United States rather than import.

The great majority of the Northern people believed slavery to be evil, and had, therefore, two reasons for opposing slavery in the new territory west of the Mississippi. They were:
(one) They objected to slavery because they thought it would seriously injure that part of the country.
(two) They objected to slavery because if the new territory should be admitted as slave states, the South would thereby gain in number of representatives in Congress, and would have a larger majority than those states in the North. Giving the south section a majority of votes would strengthen and expand slavery, and, at the same time secure the passage of laws which would permit the free importation of all kinds of manufactured goods from Europe.

The South, on the other hand, was firmly convinced that its prosperity depended upon the extension of slave labor and free trade with Europe. The people from the South saw that the North was rapidly outstripping them in growth of population. If then, the new territory should come in as free states, the result would be that the North would then get control of Congress, and so control trade.

Both sides were more than eager, because since 1812 five states-- Louisiana, Indiana, Mississippi, Illinois and Alabama--had entered the union. This made the number of free and slave states equal, with each section having eleven. The next state admitted would throw the power on the side of either free or slave. So now, when Missouri took steps to gain admission as a slave state, the South urged the measure with all its might, and the North fought against it "tooth and nail."

A compromise was struck, and Missouri was to be allowed to enter the union as a slave state, but on the express condition that in all future cases the states formed out of the territory should come in free. Congress passed this law in 1820 under the name of the Missouri Compromise.

Meanwhile, Maine entered the Union in 1821, so that when Missouri also entered the union that meant the balance between the free and the slave states was still kept. Each section had twelve states.

Most thought that the slavery question was settled "forever." But the fact remained that it continued on for nearly twenty-five years, and became more dangerous as it continued. The fire was fueled by groups in Saint Louis and other Southern interests.

At the time the compromise was made it was solemnly declared that it would stand "forever." "Forever" wasn't "Forever," and the South demanded the right to carry slavery into the region of Nebraska, beyond Missouri.

In 1854, a law was proposed by Steven A. Douglas (Senator, Illinois). This was the bill entitled the Kansas and Nebraska Bill. This was just two years before the completion of the railroad bridge.

This bill cut what was then the territory of Nebraska into two parts. The southern portion was called Kansas. It was left to the settlers of these two territories to decide whether they would have slave labor or not. Congress passed the bill, and thus repealed the Missouri agreement made in 1820. The North was indignant at the new law. The race was on for the settlement and possession of Kansas.

No sooner had President Pierce signed the Kansas-Nebraska Bill, than bands of armed men poured into the territory resolved to win it either by fraud or by force. The violence started in 1854, and the struggle to gain control from both parties deservedly earned the name of "Bleeding Kansas." The sympathizers from both sides busily engaged in every way to import their own into the territory by means of steamboats from the South, and in the future, by the new and expanded railroad potential from the North. (Therefore this bridge at Rock Island was a key factor for both interests. One that the South would like eliminated and the North worked feverishly to have completed.)

Now! The location of the first bridge crossing the Mississippi River was becoming more important to both sides, as its location would favor that section where the bridge was placed.

On July 18, 1853 Jefferson Davis, now Secretary of War in

Pierce's cabinet, spoke to a Philadelphia audience on the subject of a railroad which he proposed should be built from Memphis to California by the extreme southern route. Davis was doubtlessly interested in a transcontinental railroad by the southern route as a means of linking the far West to the South.

His Southern ties were strong, and he was greatly disturbed by the progress and speed at which the wheels of a Northern railroad were spinning across the plains of Illinois, its tracks pointed toward Council Bluffs by crossing the Mississippi River at Rock Island.
Davis could, as Secretary of War, find reason for advocating a railroad to the Pacific. It would be in the national interest. The railroad would be essential to the national defense and would require a bridge over the Mississippi at some point, preferably at Saint Louis or Memphis.
Davis would certainly have favored a more southerly crossing by the Southern Pacific.

Jefferson Davis was quoted "...stop that damned Rock Island bridge. It's bound to help those infernal Yankees on the way to Nebraska and the Pacific."

Until this time, the South had generally controlled the government. The period from the beginning of Washington's first term until the Civil War was seventy-two years. During that time, Southern-born presidents had been elected for terms amounting altogether to fifty-two years, while only five Northern presidents had been elected for one term each, or twenty years total. The South knew that the North had increased so much faster in population. The Republican party (which the South nicknamed in early 1856 the "Black Republicans") was opposed to holding the black man in bondage. It was growing so rapidly that it would soon be in control. Free-state men denounced the opposite party as "Border Ruffians." The "Border Ruffians" called the free-state men "Abolitionists" and as stated before "Black Republicans."

One of the "most notorious" Abolitionists was John Brown, a descendant of Peter Brown, who came over on the Mayflower in 1620. When he was a boy, John witnessed a slave boy cruelly beaten by his master and vowed "eternal war with slavery." In 1855, he went to Kansas to take up the battle to make that territory a free state, and also to strike a blow at slavery.

In 1852 a book was published called "Uncle Tom's Cabin," written by Harriet Beecher Stone. It clearly was the catalyst for the Civil War. It showed the worst of slavery, and increased strong opposition to the slavery cause.

The North accelerated their resistance to letting the Southern section have control by attacking Southern slave owners through publications, books and speeches. This stirred migration into the two territories of Kansas and Nebraska. As most were from Northern states, access would be by crossing the Mississippi at Rock Island, Illinois, and Davenport, Iowa. The bridge was much to the displeasure of Jefferson Davis.

Another opposing force against the railroad bridge at Rock Island-Davenport was the city of Saint Louis. Many groups were organized and many meetings were held in protest to the construction of the bridge at Rock Island. The city supported Jefferson Davis's idea of a railroad westward from Memphis to the Pacific, crossing the Mississippi by way of Saint Louis.

Therefore, an intense rivalry between Chicago and Saint Louis ensued. As Saint Louis was nearly three times the size of the "Windy City," it was enjoying a monopoly in Western commerce. The Chamber of Commerce "resolved" that a bridge was unconstitutional, that it was a dangerous obstruction to navigation. They declared it was the duty of every Western state, river city and town to take immediate action to prevent the erection of such a structure. A resolution also was passed by the city of Saint Louis to apply to the Supreme Court of the United States for an injunction, restraining the building of the bridge at Rock Island.

The bridge definitely had enemies who were actively engaged in keeping it from being placed at Rock Island .

The United States Court, on a technicality threw out the protest of the Saint Louis merchants, and other persons interested in defeating the Rock Island placement of the bridge. These groups joined forces to resort to any means to stop the Rock Island bridge- even forgetting moral and ethical values to stop it.

Murder being no exception.

CHAPTER FOUR: AN ATTEMPT TO BURN THE BRIDGE BY BOATMEN

The Colonel was brutally murdered and two years later the decision was made. The first bridge over the Mississippi River was to be built at Rock Island. The very site finally chosen was where the Colonel had established his trading post and wanted so desperately to have the bridge established in his territory.

May fourth, eighteen hundred and fifty six, when the Carson docked at Rock Island, its crew had learned about two incidents pertaining to the bridge before it was built. It seemed that one night this "Big Joe" fellow decided he would take it upon himself to burn the bridge. He had tried to recruit a group of men to help him. After much persuasion, two others accepted the challenge. The boat people called the leader "Big Joe," but he did have a real name, Joe Piaza. He was a large, outspoken, arrogant type who could only see things his way and only knew how to do things in a destructive, revengeful or violent manner. He was thought to have been involved in the Colonel's murder in some way, but somehow escaped prosecution.

Because of the extreme darkness on the night he and his friends chose to make their attempt, their efforts were thwarted, and the fire was extinguished without causing any damage. He and his friends were caught and jailed. Later, they were out on bail, paying only a small fine.

"Another more recent happening in an effort to destroy the bridge only a few days ago involved some of the local riverboat people," Brickle recalled.

This second attempt occurred when a watchman on the wooden bridge had heard a suspicious noise at the second span from the Iowa side. He hastened to see what it was. Two men dropped from the bridge into a skiff below, and made off into the darkness. When the watchman reached the span where they had been, he found already in place a lighted fuse, about to set fire to a large pile of ignitable materials including oakum and laths. Resin, tar, turpentine saltpeter and oil were all arranged for causing a fire.

The watchman quickly stomped out and extinguished the punk and threw everything into the churning water below. The perpetrators escaped into the darkness and were not apprehended. Many names were suggested but with no proof. The skiff was never found. Word spread concerning these attempts. However, it seemed for now that the bridge was safe in Rock Island.

One chance to stop it...contact Bob Birch.

Bob Birch, a notorious criminal and member of the "Banditti" of the Mississippi River, was contacted and soon made a trip to Saint Louis to meet with a group of men thought to be opposed to the bridge now that it was in place. This group of outlaws roamed up and down both sides of the river doing deeds for whoever would pay for their unlawful actions. Birch left with instructions to do whatever could be done to destroy the bridge. He later was convicted as one of the planners of Colonel Davenport's murder. Therefore no chance for him to do harm to the bridge.

All the concerns of the South seemed to continually try to find a way to put the bridge out of action.

CHAPTER FIVE:
TAKING ON
A RAPIDS PILOT

Philip Suiter rose early this May fifth in order to meet Glynn Bright, a LeClaire friend, who was going to Davenport on business by horse and buggy. Philip had been hired by Captain Brickle to pilot the J.B. Carson from the Rock Island levee up through the rapids to LeClaire, Iowa. Glynn Bright had told Philip he could ride along with him on his way to Davenport . The trip was a good two hour ride along the Mississippi. It was a beautiful twenty-five miles. Philip enjoyed the trip on land because he could relax, without the responsibility of being on the river as a pilot running the rapids. Sitting back and enjoying the ride, he

could also check out the rapids from a different perspective. A trip like this now and then was beneficial. Boats coming down from the north always picked up their pilots at LeClaire, down by the big old "Green Tree"," slightly down river from the LeClaire Hotel.
Northbound boats wanted pilots aboard at Rock Island or Davenport, giving the crew time to organize and prepare for the rough ride into the rapids. The pilot became captain for this part of the trip.

The J.B. Carson, docked at Rock Island, had offered to send a skiff to the Davenport levee to pick up Philip. Philip declined because he thought he'd like to walk the new bridge. Philip had chosen to leave his LeClaire friend and carriage at the point where the new bridge ended on the Iowa side, saying he wanted to walk the new bridge to the Illinois side.

"It wouldn't be any trouble at all to take you to the Davenport levee," Bright told Philip.

"Thanks anyway, Glynn, but I'd like to walk across the bridge. Thanks for the ride", he said gratefully.

The ride had been rough because of the ruts in the roadway caused by the recent rains and runoffs. A boat ride would seem tame compared to the muddy, bumpy, buggy ride. Stepping out of the carriage, Philip started for the bridge approach. He had to climb a steep incline to get up the embankment onto the bridge roadway. The slope was created so it would meet the bridge at the same elevation, with a gentler incline coming off the bridge. The ramp continued down to solid ground, giving the trains a gradual downhill grade coming off the bridge.

It was about a half mile from one end of the bridge to the other. It wasn't an easy walk. Your steps had to be spaced to acquire a rhythm of the distance between the railroad ties mounted on the base floor of the bridge. Philip made the crossing onto the Illinois side where he could see the J.B. Carson docked at the Rock Island levee. Anxious to climb on board with his friend Captain Brickle, he bounded up the gangway, and saluted his old friend. Both extended their hands for a mutually warm greeting.

"How've you been?" he asked the Captain.

"Fine!" Brickle replied. "Seen that lawyer gal lately?" he grinned.

"Once in a while, whenever I'm down this way. I'd like to see her more often. She's quite a lady," he smiled.

Philip had, on one of his trips, become acquainted with a young lady he met when she stopped him to ask questions about the boat he was about to board. She was most interested and asked just about everything you could ask concerning the big boats. A friendship developed, and they had become _good_ friends.

Early on the morning of May sixth, 1856, the wintery sky light had not yet given way to the easterly glow which was expected to break over the dark gray overcast. The howling wind of the night before had subsided somewhat, but still sent dark moving patches cascading across the water of the great river. The wind was scattering papers and trash from the gatherings of the bridge protestors the night before, strewing them about the levee shoreline. At times the groups had become quite violent and required restraint by local authorities on the Rock Island side of the Mississippi.

This morning, Captain Brickle of the J.B. Carson stepped onto the bridge to survey the serenity of the calming breezes. He turned his face into the northeast wind, squinted, and began to assess the situation.

"Looks like we might get underway this morning," he said to his pilot, Philip Suiter.

Brickle was fifty-five years old. His years on the river as a riverboat captain showed in his weathered, lined face and gave him the look of a seasoned riverboater. He was Philip's senior by twenty years. Each line bore a story of some consequence he'd rather forget.

He smiled at the thought of many incidents that would bring the average boater scurrying for cover. He knew he could tackle anything the "old man river" threw at him. He had no fear of this "Mighty One", but he highly respected its authority.

Well, maybe with one exception. He knew well that short stretch of fifteen miles just up river from his present position, now located on the south bank of the Mississippi river here at Rock Island, Illinois, could create challenges. (The river ran east and west where the Government fort and Arsenal had been established.) This section of the river could be a nightmare to riverboats without a seasoned professional pilot to navigate the dangerous, churning rapids. He shuddered at the thought of taking his boat and cargo through this part of the river without a rapids pilot. Hence, the hiring of a rapids pilot, Phillip Suiter, from LeClaire, Iowa. No point in taking chances.

Captain Brickle had become fascinated by this location of the river and had given thought to perhaps making it his home one day. He'd given thought to learning to run the rapids himself and becoming one of these esteemed rapids pilots.

His interest had been brought on by one of his recent passages through this area when he picked up a pilot several years back. Because of weather, he had been forced to spend a few days at LeClaire, Iowa, where most of these dashing rapids pilots resided in their elegant homes of Victorian splendor. Their dress matched their residences and personalities. Self-confident and gallant. During his stay in the LeClaire Hotel, where the pilots would gather and fraternize in the lobby, exchanging tales of great spine-chilling experiences on the "great one," he had sat and listened to their often exaggerated stories and had watched them play "the game" together. He was overwhelmed by the object of "the game" -its useful method of teaching and informing. It passed the waiting hours when the pilots weren't piloting a boat or raft through the rapids.

"The game" was played sitting around a large wooden box filled with sand. The river pilots, sitting around the box dressed in their finery with the air and grace of aristocratic princes, took turns drawing in the sand with ornate magnificent canes the outline of some part of the river boundary, detailing islands, jettys, shallow water and any other identifying characteristic clues to that portion of the river of which the participant had drawn. When he finished, the viewers would, based on their knowledge of the river, guess the location of that part of the river, thus completing a round of "the game." Another leader took his turn trying to stump the others.

There were men whom Captain Brickle had heard of in his many trips up and down the river. Their reputations were known far and wide. There were men like Julius Suiter and Captain Orrin Smith, and there were many other well known river pilots of this part of the river.

Brickle had become friends with the young Philip Suiter during his stay with the elder Suiter. The son was descendant following in the footsteps of a grandfather and his father. Captain Brickle became very close to the young man and had chosen him for his trips in this part of the river, especially through the treacherous rapids.

Suiter had already come aboard the night before. He was

only 35 years old but was "river wise," and had made many trips up and down the river, especially through the rapids area (on both boats and rafts). A dashing, ruddy-faced, weather-beaten riverman, he had learned the ways of the river from his father, Julius, and a grandfather long departed.

He liked working the boats from Rock Island. It gave him time to visit the young lady he had met in Rock Island. She was the daughter of one of the big investors of the Chicago and Rock Island Railroad. She was a petite, young, attractive, brunette who had been in Rock Island only two years after completing law school in the East. (Yale, no less). She was not like other women he had known--much more interesting and she definitely was smart.

Her name was Virginia Sheffield.

She had watched the rift between the boat people and the railroad, and had been very vocal herself concerning the advantages of crossing the river by rail. She and Philip had gotten to know each other, and had many discussions concerning the bridge dispute. Although Philip had been brought up to think the river was the most important means of transportation in this area, he had to admit that she was very convincing with her railroad argument and he liked her spirited attitude.

Once she had marched into the middle of a group of protestors and given her little railroad lecture on the benefits of supporting the railroad bridge.
Philip was impressed and hoped that the really angry

protestors would only listen to her comments and not get ugly. She was telling them what they didn't want to hear.

Their relationship at this time had been mostly curiosity. Neither had had much exposure to each other's backgrounds. She was intrigued and anxious to learn more about these river people because her knowledge of boating had been solely associated with friends of her father who spent time boating on eastern sailing ships and yachts.

There was a definite difference.

Philip's was an occasional meeting with lawyers who had been aboard steamboats on which he had worked, on their way to a business meeting with some northern companies up river who were requesting legal help in pursuit of their businesses. They liked to be on the bridge where he was piloting the steamboat through the rapids. They asked lots of questions and became very friendly. They made Philip feel important.

Once, while on a trip down river and during a stop in New Boston, there was a tall, lanky guy hanging around the dock. He said his name was "Abe". He said he liked to come down by the river. It was just a short walk from his office in downtown New Boston. The river gave him a good place to contemplate cases on which he was working. He, too, was a lawyer. An Illinois lawyer.

This girl, Virginia Sheffield, sure was on Philip's mind a lot. She had an unusual interest in what was taking place here along the river in Rock Island. Most of the ladies he had known couldn't care less. They spent their time in their homes and with their families.

CHAPTER SIX:
THE WEATHER APPEARS TO BE LETTING UP

The wind was still blowing but not with the intensity of the night before.

The new railroad bridge spanned between Rock Island, Illinois, and Davenport, Iowa. The main span ran from the government-owned seat or fort and arsenal to the Iowa side at Davenport. It was an important facility in case of war- which seemed to be brewing on the horizon.

The bridge was to be the newest east-west link for the railroads. No longer would they have to unload trainloads of cargo at Rock Island, then reload onto riverboats and take their cargo down to Saint Louis, only to unload and reload onto trains again in order to go cross country into the western territory. It had meant repeating the same procedures at the Missouri River.

Now the trains could go cross country without delays.

Today, the gray wooden bridge stood ghostlike against the Davenport hillsides, lighted only from the dismal early gray spring day that saw only tinges of green to indicate a seasonal change was on its way.

Captain Brickle thought to himself that even though the wind was lighter today, the fierce current of the river seemed to move in a way that combined with the dreariness of the day. This could create big problems getting through and into the upper, more rapid part of the river on the other side of the bridge.

The river seemed to swirl a dreadful warning in the water as it rushed by the bow of the J.B. Carson.
High water from the early spring thaws and rains had been the main delay for the boats running the first new railroad bridge crossing the "Mighty Mississippi."

Brickle wondered, "Would it be a race to be the first one through?"

There were some eager captains raring to get underway and be the first. Prestige and a place in history were at stake. Boats lay waiting with the J.S. Carson, like the Tishomingo, the Kate Paulding, the Hamburg, the Clara Dean, the Mattie Wayne, the Ben Bolt and the Effie Afton. All were carrying perishable goods aboard, reason enough to be the first one through. The Effie Afton was no different. She was a large, brand new boat with a large cargo of freight, passengers and livestock. The Effie Afton crew was anxious to have the maiden voyage behind them.

Brickle noticed a great deal of activity aboard the Effie Afton. She also was getting steam up as if she were ready to shove off.

Captain Brickle shook out the pipe that he had been clenching between his teeth and had occasionally removed with his thumb and forefinger. This unconscious gesture seemed to help when he was in the thought process of decision making. Specifically-

"Was it time to run the bridge?"

He ended up with a hand on the bridge rail...the pipe stem pointing almost directly at what it was he was contemplating, in this case the newly constructed railroad bridge.

"The northeast wind would be a slight crosswind off the port bow," he assured himself.

He felt because of the wind direction, his boat should have

priority for getting underway. With that, the confidence seemed to swell within him, and he moved to the starboard side of the bridge, where several of the deckhands stood waiting casually around the capstan. (A capstan is a machine for moving or lifting by means of a heavy cable around a vertical spindle mounted drum that is rotated manually or by steam power, and is generally mounted on the forward deck.) The crew were exchanging reports which they had overheard the night before or had been told by some of the other deckhands from the other waiting boats. The most excited of the group told of a plan he had overheard about a great vengeance against the new bridge by the boat people, and of the possible destruction of the bridge that was to take place soon.

The bridge definitely had enemies.

Many of the Carson crew had watched in amazement the actions and threats of the protestors who hated the bridge and the railroad so badly they had themselves worked up into a frenzy. They not only had contempt for railroads, but especially for any railroad that ran over the river where they worked their boats. They felt the cargoes of the world should be carried by steamboats. They believed their livelihoods were in jeopardy.

The Pilot Philip Suiter had strolled onto the bridge and was preparing busily to be underway, He nodded approvingly to the captain.

"Morning, Captain,", he saluted with the flair of a veteran river pilot. "Kinda looks like we'll do it today," he said, addressing the Captain.

"Could be so!...Could be so!" answered Captain Brickle.

CHAPTER SEVEN: THE EFFIE AFTON HITS THE BRIDGE AND BURNS

"Prepare to cast off," Captain Brickle ordered.

"Aye...aye...Captain," quickly responded the second mate.

A second order followed. "We'll free the stern and hold the bow until we have steam up."

"Aye Capt'n," the man acknowledged.

By now the Effie Afton had already dropped her lines, and was starting to pull away from her mooring. She had her flag flying at the jack staff. She wasn't up to full steam, but was not concerned if she was hindering the Carson or anyone else as she accidentally rammed into one of the other boats. Causing very little or no damage, she continued on her way. The Carson was up to steam and also already underway. It seemed that the Effie Afton was intent on being the first through the bridge.

The two boats now were running side by side with the Effie Afton pulling away from the J.S. Carson. The Carson was not at full throttle, and being the first through wasn't a big deal to Brickle. He was stunned to see the Effie Afton steam off at full throttle ahead of his boat. Philip, now the pilot, averted to the north to avoid the Afton's wake putting them farther behind.

Loud bells, whistles, and cheering interrupted Captain Brickle's thoughts as the J.B. Carson was making way from the Rock Island levee. He wondered why the Effie Afton had gotten underway so fast, and why she was so intent on beating him and the J.S. Carson to the bridge. The bridge revolving span had opened, and the bridge was ready to except the first boat passing through.

Now the protestors on shore were all excited, watching the two boats underway. The Afton was at the bridge. Brickle could see something was happening upriver at the new railroad bridge. He was now only a few hundred yards away from the bridge and the Effie Afton. He could hear the shouting from spectators along the Rock Island shore who were pointing and cheering something about the bridge. He could determine that most were cheering jubilantly.

Brickle turned himself upriver, facing the distant bridge as the Carson was rapidly getting close to the bridge, and just behind the Effie Afton. Now he could see the Effie Afton was ajar inside the revolving, swing portion of the bridge.

Something didn't seem right to him!

The cheering, the bells and the whistles grew louder and louder. He ordered his pilot to head straight toward the bridge, where it appeared the Effie Afton seemed to be in some kind of trouble. Perhaps she had become attached to one of the bridge piers. As the Carson got closer it was obvious that the Afton had hit the bridge and was swinging her stern sideways into the stationary pier. The current and the wind were not helping the situation, creating a potential disaster.

Captain Brickle heard a loud crunching sound... now he knew what was happening. The Effie Afton had misjudged the currents, and had gotten caught in the eddies near the big pier and swung into it. She now was at the mercy of the river as it pushed her violently up against the new bridge. Next, he heard the screams of the third deck passengers, who in the confusion were panicking, and running crazily about the deck. He recognized the cries of the animals occupying the lower deck. He heard the cry of a bellowing calf calling out to its mother. The lurching and jerking of the Afton was causing chaos throughout the entire craft. Suddenly the boat keeled to its starboard side, and the passengers were crowding frantically to make their way to port side.

Brickle told the crew to make ready to tie onto the Afton, to help the passengers find their way down from the upper passenger decks, and direct them to the rail where the J.S. Carson was ready to bring them aboard.

As the Afton made another violent lurch, more screams came from the passengers not able to get to the port side. The Afton rolled farther, and many of the passengers were thrown into the churning, bleak, black water. The animals had broken through the rails and were thrown into the water on top of and amongst the shivering and drowning passengers. Some of the animals were thrashing and submerging in an effort of survival. People thrown into the water fought to find floating debris they thought was stable enough for them to climb onto. The mashing and pounding was causing people to be rendered unconscious, and some disappeared into the dark cold waters. Many were not to be seen again.

One of the passengers retrieved from the upper deck of the Afton was Susan Smith. Once she had calmed down she told her rescuers that she was on her way upriver with her daughter, Joy, to Galena to meet her husband, John, who had been hired by the Territorial Lead Company to design and oversee the construction of shot towers. (This was a unique method for making lead bullets. It was done by dropping molten lead from a high tower and as the lead pellets fell through the air they would cool into round balls to be used as ammunition for firearms.)

This had become a major industry as the threats of war were becoming more and more a threat to the nation.

Susan Smith had said, "Everything we own was on the Effie Afton."

By now flames were encompassing the two top decks rising up almost beyond the stacks. Over-turning kerosene heating stoves were sprewing kerosene onto the hot coals, spreading fire throughout the Effie Afton.

The crowd on shore was cheering louder than ever when the flames spread to the bridge timbers and the deck structure. They showed no remorse for the terrible disaster and loss of lives taking place on the river. Their only concern seemed to be that this new threat to their own futures was being removed.

Once all the passengers who could be found were safely on board the J.S. Carson, Captain Brickle gave orders to shove off away from the Effie Afton and the Rock Island bridge. The sky was turning brilliant red-orange as the fire was now reflecting on the black, swirling current. Flames were spreading onto the bridge deck, spreading fire over the railroad bed, platform, feeding on the creosote coating. Flames shot even higher than the stacks of the Afton before they plummeted into the water.

Still the horns, the bells, the whistles and the shouts of joy kept coming from the many spectators on the shore. The smell of burning flesh and animals left a putrid odor drifting onto the J.S. Carson as it pulled away from the Effie Afton. Then, suddenly, a portion of revolving section of the burning bridge collapsed. Its timbers fell on the disabled and burning

Effie Afton. The force released the Afton from its trapped inferno and she went swirling in the current as a floating pyre down river.

Captain Brickle gave the order.
"Philip, let's put in back at Rock Island and see if we can do anything else to help the passengers."

He put a blanket about the shoulders of one of the Afton passengers they had taken off the distressed boat. He was holding the shivering young lady who was clutching her daughter to her chest. "We'll see that you get to Galena to be with your husband as soon as possible," he assured her.

When finally docked again, Philip joined Brickle on the main deck. They could see the frantic, fevered turmoil going up and down the shore. Philip could make out the young lady, Virginia Sheffield, in the midst of a group of protestors who were celebrating so exuberantly. He could see that she was scolding them because they were cheering this dreadful event. That "big fella" Joe was right in her face, shaking his fist at her violently. When Philip saw this he ran down the gangplank and headed toward the crowd where Virginia was now surrounded by a raging group of rousters. He pushed one of the protestors out of the way and moved in next to Virginia. His main concern was he wanted to get her out of there...fast.

Big Joe stepped up to him and demanded. "What side are you on, Mister Pilot?" he yelled at Philip.
"You're a boatman, ain't ya?" He again demanded.

"Yes, I'm a boatman, but this situation doesn't justify this kind of violence."

The answer brought an ugly frown to the big man's face. His forehead turned a bright red. He was beginning to blow through his nostrils and his eyes moved up into the top of his head, sending a frightening signal that he was about to lunge at Philip any second.

Philip held his ground and again motioned Virginia out of the way, in case the big man did make a move toward him. Philip was not afraid. On several occasions he had encountered many drunks and ruffians who just didn't like his looks. He had fought several times before in unpleasant situations like this.

Quietly, almost whispering, he told Virginia to make her way out of the circle of protestors. Virginia was a determined young lady and not terribly concerned about the danger that appeared imminent.

"Please, Virginia, go now. I'll handle this!" Philip insisted.

Next he heard, "I know who you are...you're one of those "big shot" river pilots from up at LeClaire over on the Iowa side-ain't ya?" questioned the big fella Joe. "You don't care if we all lose our jobs workin' the boats-do ya?"

He continued his line of questioning, raising his voice with every word. He was getting more and more like he was wanting a fight, almost begging for it.

"You're right, I am one of the river pilots from LeClaire," Philip answered calmly.

This surprised the big man.
Big Joe didn't understand why this guy wasn't shaking in his boots.

"We river pilots don't want you to lose your jobs! We don't believe it'll happen as there will always be a need for people working the boats," he said.
"If you would just calm down and think about what this lady is trying to tell you, you would see the potential for even more jobs here on the river when the railroads start moving shipments into the new territory from all parts east of the Mississippi."

These words were far from music to this roaring, frantic, fist-shaking man, itching to get it on with Philip.

"Hold on there!" A booming voice could be heard from just outside the ring of protestors.

Suddenly breaking into the middle of the circled group was Captain Brickle.

"What's going on here?" he demanded as he stepped between the "big man" Joe and Philip. "This doesn't solve anything," he exclaimed.
" Joe, take your boys...go get a drink and cool down. This isn't the time for violence. Don't you know there's been a

disaster here?"

Brickle knew this big "Joe fella" because of a fracas a few years back when one of his crew members had a confrontation with Joe over the placement of some unloaded cargo. When Brickle stepped in to separate the two, Joe had hit him with the end of a heavy, wet mooring line used to secure and tie up the large steamers.

Brickle realized what was happening as he saw " Joe" coming at him a second time swinging the end of the mooring line. Brickle responded in time to duck the blow and to lay a "haymaker" on the side of Joe's head knocking him to the ground rendering him totally unconscious.

Joe remembered the previous situation all too well. He didn't want to get into it with this guy again. So he started to back away telling his boys that this wasn't finished and would be continued another day.

"I'll pick the time," Joe rambled on.

Philip, relieved, retreated and caught up with Virginia. Turning his head back toward Brickle he smiled and said,

"Thanks, Captain, I owe ya one. See you later."

Then turning to Virginia, "Lady, no more confrontations with the likes of these ruffians...you could get yourself killed." Philip was grinning as he pretended to scold her.

"Thanks, Philip, I didn't know you cared," she kidded him back.

"Well, I do, and I don't want to see you get hurt."

"Since you won't be going north today or until they have the channel cleared, let's go to my house. I want you to meet my father," she invited.

"Ok. First I must let Captain Brickle know what I'm doing."

They walked toward the J.S. Carson and up to the gangplank where Brickle had returned. He was already standing in his typical pose leaning on the rail with his pipe between his fingers, as he pointed to the two coming aboard. He thought it a good idea for Philip to go with her and meet her father.

The two started toward town to where the residences were, a little past what was the business district. Virginia directed Philip to a big Victorian house where she lived. They could still hear the shouting from the protestors.
One of the slogans the protestors were chanting was:

> *"Shovel up that furnace,*
> *'Til smoke puts out the stars,*
> *We've just been built a riverboat,*
> *To whip the railroad cars."*

A big iron gate led into the massive front yard that led to the front entrance of the house. Virginia, opening the door, showed Philip into the foyer.

"Father, I'm home." she announced. "And I want you to meet a friend I have with me."

Virginia and her father lived in one of the finest areas of Rock Island. Their home was of the Victorian style, and was located just a short distance from where the railroad tracks made the turn to the approach onto the bridge. The home was well appointed and all the furnishings were of the highest quality and were well chosen by someone of good taste.

Virginia's mother had died from cholera and Virginia had moved here with her father after graduating from law school at Yale. Mr. Sheffield was a director of the Southern Railroad, which ran from and to Chicago. In the early fifties, Sheffield and Farmun had completed construction of the Michigan Southern Railroad to Chicago, which was just a preface to the building of the Chicago, Rock Island and Pacific Railroad to the Mississippi River. Sheffield, along with Henry Farnam, and with the aid of Eastern capitalists and investors, had sponsored earlier projects. Together a group of men in Iowa and Illinois projected a railroad that should cross the Mississippi, traverse Iowa, and reach the banks of the Missouri at Council Bluffs. A bold plan, typical of the projects that Farnum and the capitalists associated with him had pushed to completion. They would never forget the efforts of the late Colonel Davenport.
They credited the Colonel with having paved the way for

the railroad bridge. They were all vigorous men who let nothing stand in the way of their ambitions. Railroading was enjoying amazing growth and prosperity and the surplus was theirs to invest in western expansion.

It was not difficult, in this instance, to get what they needed. The Illinois legislature authorized construction of the first span, which would extend from the town of Rock Island, on the Illinois shore, to Rock Island, the government-owned seat of a fort and arsenal. Permission to build the longest span, from the island to the Iowa shore was readily granted by the Iowa Legislature.

Opposition brought such pressure to bear in Washington that the Secretary of War ordered the U.S. District Attorney for northern Illinois to apply for an injunction to prevent construction of the railroad across Rock Island near the government's fort. After lengthy argument, the presiding Judge, John McLean, an Associate Justice of the Supreme Court, denied the injunction the government had wanted. The case of the United States vs. The Railroad Bridge Company was decided in July of 1855 in favor of the bridge, and from that date construction was pushed ahead at top speed.

Virginia's father had played a major part in the entire scheme and operation of obtaining the bridge.

"Father, did you hear that one of the boats hit and set fire to the bridge?" she asked.

"Yes, one of the men came by just shortly after it happened and gave me the tragic news. It's very bad for all of us. There will be much made of it before it's settled. We'll get the bridge back up and ready as soon as we can."

After much discussion concerning the recent event down by the docks, Philip learned from Virginia's father that he was very distressed concerning the outcry that arose from many of the steamboaters who claimed that the bridge virtually put an end to navigation of the upper river. Philip was not one of these rivermen, as he saw the bridge could only mean growth for the country and new horizons for the rivermen. Pleasantries ensued and they retired to the parlor.

Mr. Sheffield stirred the fire, looked up at Philip and asked,

"Virginia tells me you are a pilot on the river?"

"That's so," Philip answered. "I have been for twelve years...I love the river. Our families have been river people since they came to America, three generations ago," he added.

"Well, as you know we are from the East. The Sheffields were in textiles. I got interested in railroading, and made investments in the railroad line running from Chicago to here at Rock Island. I believe the future is in railroading. Moving goods cross country by rail and, of course, by steamboats which bring the goods to the railroads. I believe the two should work harmoniously together.
I understand there is some concern here that it can't work".

Philip answered, " There have been some protestors and some gatherings in opposition to the new bridge. Many river people don't want a bridge crossing the Mississippi. By the way, it was the Effie Afton, a brand new steamboat on her maiden voyage, who destroyed the revolving section of the bridge. The Effie Afton was also destroyed. Many of the passengers survived, although I believe some were lost along with much of the livestock on board."

"I was piloting the J.B. Carson. We started for the span when the Effie Afton walked past us like she was going to beat us to the gap and be the first one through the bridge. We decided not to pursue her and let her go by."

"She got about halfway through when we saw that her stern was caught in one of the whirlpools that eddied around the long pier. The pilot on duty made a valiant effort to hold her to a straight course, but the boat was like a leaf in the violent current being swept under the bridge."

"We saw the helpless boat driven first against one pier, then the other. The pilot thought for an instant he might save her, but the rushing water drove her a third time onto the pier. We then heard a fearful crash, and the screams of the passengers who were thrown out of their berths, half naked and frightened."

"That final crash lodged the Effie Afton against the starboard pier, causing her to careen at an angle of forty-five degrees, the water swirling over her hold. We thought she must go over any moment. Fortunately, the Effie Afton was lodged in such a way that many of the passengers were able to escape by climbing up onto the bridge and onto the J.B. Carson. Upper deck passengers scrambled onto the Carson once we were in position to take them aboard. We cleared her of her passengers and crew in a remarkably short time. I heard reports after the disaster that at least five people had drowned. It could have been worse. We rescued all that we could." Philip said sadly.

"Terrible...Terrible!" Mr. Sullivan sighed.
"Virginia, were you there?" her father asked.

"I was on shore," Virginia replied. "Later in the day, Philip and I got into it with some of the protestors. Philip's Captain Brickle came to our rescue or it might have gotten a lot uglier than it did."

"Well, I'm glad you're both safe." He breathed a sigh of relief and stirred the logs in the fireplace.

The fire came alive, brightening everything in the room. The faces of the people shone softly from the reflection of the bristling fire. The father excused himself, and went into the adjoining room which had a large rolltop desk where stacks of papers were piled high inside the accordion cover. Philip could see this was his study and where he did his work. Shelves were lined with books that looked like volumes of legal books.

As he left he turned to Philip and said, "I'm happy to make

your acquaintance. I'll leave you two alone to visit."

He left them sitting in the great room staring at the fire. Both were sad that the day had ended so tragically.

Finally, Virginia broke the silence saying, "Philip, would you care to stay for dinner?"

Philip was not used to the word "dinner" to refer to the evening meal. His family always referred to eating a meal at this time of day as "supper." However, he wasn't much for missing a good meal regardless of what it was called.

"You're sure it wouldn't be a bother?" he asked.

"No, not at all. I'll go tell father's cook to put on another place setting. It'll give us something to talk about other than railroading," she said as she glided out of the room. Philip sensed that she was pleased that he had accepted the invitation.

He followed her with his eyes as she left the room and liked what he saw. The way she carried herself and her perky step gave away that she was full of vitality.

Dinner was one of Virginia's father's favorites; boiled catfish with all the trimmings. A nice white German wine was a welcomed treat. Philip enjoyed the conversation which was dominated by the trials of the bridge construction.
Mr. Sheffield knew the story of how Colonel Davenport was murdered. It all made sense the way Philip explained

the reason for the Colonel's murder. Philip was sure he was murdered because of his interest in getting the bridge established at Rock Island. Mr. Sheffield had never been informed as to the connection of the murderers with the stories of the Bandittis up and down the river, especially those in Saint Louis. But judging from information received from local law enforcement people he wasn't surprised. He had some dealings with some of them in respect to building the railroad bridge. They had done everything they could to stop the construction. Everything from burning supplies, to stopping shipments to the site to scaring off or buying off bridge workers.

Later, after dinner the three adjourned to the sitting room for an after-dinner cordial of Benedictine. More enjoyable conversation ensued.

Mr. Sheffield asked, "Tell me about the rapids, are they as treacherous as I have heard?"

"Well sir," Philip responded. "I've encountered some pretty hazardous situations through that part of the river. Once bringing a large raft of logs down river from Dubuque to the lumber mill in Davenport, one of the main ties to keep the raft together broke loose, letting a section do an about-face. The whole unit was unmanageable, and careening off large boulders as it was swept in and around them. Finally, the other sections began breaking apart, and were being tossed about, onto rocks. We were not able to recover them until we had cleared the rapids section of the river. It was a wild and hectic ride trying to keep from being thrown into the swirling current. When we finally got through, we were then able to gather our log cargo, put them back together and deliver it to its destination. We got an education that day about how forceful the rapids are."

Virginia asked excitedly, "Have you ever come through the rapids in a small skiff or the likes?"

"Yes, I have a small birch canoe which I love to take down the rapids. It's great sport!" he answered.

"Please, would you take me with you sometime?" she pleaded.

"If you're up to it, and your father wouldn't object, I'd be honored. But I must warn you it's not for the faint-hearted."

Philip waited to see her father's reaction. This wasn't a request the father was used to hearing. Her father raised his eyebrows in amazement, thinking his daughter may have lost her mind. Fifteen miles in the churning, raging rapids in a small birch canoe with a man he had only met just a few hours earlier wasn't his idea of a pleasure trip. However, he knew her persistence and determination to do the unthinkable. He had to believe in this river pilot and approve the inevitable. She'd find a way to do it anyway. Maybe by herself, he thought. She had this adventurous spirit about her. Must be something from her mother's side of the family. He was reminded how alike they were and how much he missed Virginia's mother.

"Yes, Father. Yes, I knew you'd approve!" Virginia was up and out of her chair with excitement.

Philip proposed, "We could take the Carson up to where my duties aboard her will be finished. I'm through when we get to LeClaire. Of course, it depends on when the bridge is cleared, and provided the weather is decent enough to take a canoe through the rapids. We could spend time with my family until conditions are good enough. You could get to know the life of a river pilot."

The rest of the evening the three chatted and exchanged pleasantries about their different life-styles and how the Sheffields chose to move to Rock Island. Mr. Sheffield offered his explanation.

"After my wife died, I needed to begin a new life. I had an interest in this new railroad company. I was very interested in its future when I was appointed to its board of directors. The company needed someone in the Midwest to oversee its operation as there was interest in crossing the Mississippi River and moving into the Northwest Territory. I liked the idea and agreed to make the move to Rock Island. Virginia also was excited about the move although she hadn't finished her education. She couldn't join me immediately, but would come as soon as she finished her schooling and law degree at Yale. That was our plan and now here we are."

Philip could see Virginia's father was very happy having his daughter with him. Time was getting late and Captain

Brickle was probably wondering what had happened to his friend and pilot. Noticing the time had passed so easily, Philip brought the conversation to a close, saying,

"I must get back to the boat. Tomorrow will be a big day. If they have the bridge debris cleared we'll probably be getting underway. Virginia, if you really want to do the rapids and can be ready to go, you can join us on the Carson up to LeClaire."

"I'll be there," she exclaimed happily.

Philip rose out of his chair to leave, thanking her father for his hospitality.

Virginia followed Philip to the door.

Philip turned and held out his hand. "Thank you, Virginia. I had a great time being with you and your father. I'll look forward to our rapids trip. See you tomorrow."

Turning toward the street he missed the first step of the porch and almost fell off the last two. "That was smart." he thought to himself as he regained his balance. He turned to see Virginia with her hand covering her mouth so as not to burst out laughing.

"Watch that first step, it's a killer," she said giggling.

Embarrassed, he made a "dumb me" gesture and started for the wrought-iron gate. The fence surrounded the entire

perimeter of the property. In the middle of the gate was a wrought-iron circle with the initial "S" filling it.
Closing the gate behind him, he glanced back at the house. Virginia was still in the doorway, giving him a final wave goodbye.

Philip started toward the levee and the J.B. Carson. He had passed several buildings, and in the gas lights noticed the daffodils and tulips were breaking through the ground in some of the garden areas along the way. Their colors stood out in the semidarkness. Closer to the docks he passed a darkened building with a recessed entrance.

Three figures stepped out from within the deepest part and approached him. The first two he didn't know, but when the third person stepped forward into the light coming from one of the corner lamps, he knew it was "Big Joe."

"Where ya goin'?" Joe blurted out.
"Bin with that mouthy, little railroad bitch, ain't ya?"

Philip tried to ignore and step around him, but the two other men grabbed his arms and twisted him to the ground. Philip was unable to get free.

Big Joe stood over him with a sneer on his face while Philip was being held. "Ya son-of-a-bitchin' fancy pants. I'll teach ya to go to the other side."

He swung a big fist that hit Philip on the side of his head. Philip felt the pain, and slumped to his knees in time to hear footsteps rushing toward him. Whistles were the last he heard as he lost consciousness. By now, Joe and his cronies were leaving the scene. A policeman was attending to Philip with a handkerchief to stop the bleeding. The gash wasn't all that bad but the blow itself had caused Philip to black out.

"You'll be all right. Where are you going?" the officer asked.

Stunned, Philip told him he was heading to the J.B. Carson down at the levee.

"You're not far. I'll see you get there okay. Did you recognize any of the men who attacked you?"

"Yes, one," Philip answered, struggling to gain coherence. "One of them looked like Joe Piaza."

"Could you be sure Joe was one of them?" the officer asked.

"Yes"

"He's been trouble for us around here for some time. We did some checking on him, and discovered he's from down around Nauvoo. He has connections with part of the Banditti band of thugs that have been terrorizing up and down the river. We get reports of their activities all the time," the officer said. "The problem is, they always have someone claiming they were somewhere else when the deed was done. They get off and are never convicted."

Helping Philip to his feet, he saw the river pilot was getting his bearings back. "This way to the boat."

By now Philip was steady and gaining his senses. They started toward the boat.

"We'll try to find this Joe, and if we do, maybe you'll identify him as your assailant."

"Maybe, but if the bridge is cleared, we'll be leaving to go north for the rapids in the morning. I'm the pilot up as far as LeClaire, Iowa."

"We'll send word to you, when we've got him. Arrangements can be made at that time."

"There's talk that he was part of the Judge Fox, Birch, John and Aron Long Banditti gang. Most of them have already been convicted of Colonel Davenport's murder. We suspect he had something to do with the murder."

Arriving at the Carson, Philip thanked the officer for his timely appearance and welcomed help. He climbed up the gangway onto the boat. Captain Brickle met him as he entered the pilot house.

"Want to tell me what happened, Philip?"

Philip related the entire happenings since he had left the

Sheffields and had seen Brickle during the incident with the circle of protestors that also included Joe Piaza.

"I found we have a crew member aboard who is from Nauvoo. He said he had known this Joe. Met him when he was doing some fishing down by Pontoosuc. Said he bragged to him about being one of the so called Banditti's. Saw him living in a tent along the shore there. Had a strong smell of booze when our guy talked to him."

"Get that cut cleaned and attended to and get some rest. We may get underway tomorrow if everything is cleared and the weather cooperates."

"Aye, Aye, Sir," Philip happily agreed.

CHAPTER EIGHT:
A CLUE FOUND
ON THE WRECKAGE

The owner and officer in charge of the Effie Afton, J.S. Hurd, rounded up as many of his crew members as he could find. Everyone expressed their thoughts about the disaster. Mister Hurd wanted to get their opinions as to why and how the tragedy occurred. Captain James Parker, the pilot, had been found among the protestors stating his case against the bridge.

With everyone assembled, Hurd started the inquisition.

"Well, what happened?" he asked abruptly and sadly.

At first no response. The crew members looked at each other, waiting for someone to break the silence, for someone with the simple explanation for what had caused the tragedy.

Finally, Captain Parker spoke up.

"I was at the wheel and as we approached the gap and got into the current where heavy steering was required, I suddenly realized I had no control over the boat. As we entered the open span between the two larger sections of the bridge I felt the boat swing toward one of the piers, then veer to starboard into one of the other piers. It was swept there by the current and I had no control over its course. We were like a chip in the violent current sweeping under the bridge. I thought she might have saved herself, but the rushing water drove her a final time onto the pier on her starboard side. Couldn't hold her!" he cried out.

A lot of voices broke the silence in agreement with him.

"Couldn't be helped, that damn bridge. That's what caused it," they agreed almost in unison.

Then one of the engine maintenance men spoke up. "Mr. Hurd, Sir! Did you employ a new man to work in the engine room with us? We had someone show up the evening back saying he'd be joining us on the trip up North. He came aboard, and messed around in the engine room for a while. Some of us went up on the main deck to help some of the foreign passengers stow their belongings and get the livestock bedded down. When we returned to the engine room the new hand was nowhere to be seen."

"No, I haven't hired any new crew members since we left Portsmouth, Ohio," he said, puzzled.

"Did you take on anyone new?" he asked Captain Parker.

"No, Sir?" Parker replied.

Both men looked puzzled at this strange question before them.

Another crewman blurted out. "Sir, the last time I saw this guy he was messing around the steerage mechanism. He had a bag with some tools with him. He told me he was making some adjustment on the rudder. Later he took the bag and told me he was going ashore to get some parts. He never returned, to my knowledge. I thought it was a little strange for him to come aboard, doing things without first discussing it with any one of us, then leaving to get something for the boat without first asking us what the procedure was for making purchases for the boat. I didn't know what he was doing. It did seem strange to me at the time."

Hurd mulled this information over in his head. Could it be the Effie Afton had been sabotaged?

This was something he'd have to look into as soon as they could locate the sunken remains of the boat. Hurd knew of a man who lived in these parts who was a diver. In the morning he'd see if he could contact this man and get him to dive on the wreck and examine the steering mechanism to be sure it hadn't been tampered with.

This certainly put a different wrinkle in the situation.

In any event, the boat was lost.

Everything Captain Hurd had was invested in this beautiful river boat. He felt responsible to the other investors. He would have to explore every possible reason for this accident.

But first, on his agenda in the morning, was to contact the corporate lawyer, T.D. Lincoln of Cincinnati, and give him details to date concerning the loss of the Effie Afton. He also needed to contact certain backers in Saint Louis. May sixth would be a busy and hectic day as the news would spread fast throughout the territory.

Brickle strode across the deck of the Carson contemplating the events of the day. Especially that of the Effie Afton affair.

"No casualties! Wishful thinking!" Brickle thought.

"I saw several people disappear into that bleak, cold water with some of the animals thrashing around them.

Don't know how they could have survived."

Captain Brickle shook his head, and tried to visualize all that would be affected by this tragedy.

He thought, "The poor young wife on her way to Ganena with her daughter, ready to set up a new home and future in a strange new place had nothing but the clothes on their backs."

There would be many legal ramifications of this terrible disaster which was meant to be the start of a new and promising opportunity for the people of the river- the railroad-the chance to move into the new territories of the West.

CHAPTER NINE :
SABOTAGE OR ACCIDENT

J.S. Hurd was busy the next morning of May the sixth, getting off messages to those he felt necessary to inform about the loss of the Effie Afton. He rose early to find the telegraph office, in order to send wires to the investors and the lawyer. It wasn't hard to find, as it was next to the Fink, Walker & Company, a stage coach office in downtown Rock Island. The man behind the cage in the telegraph office was very helpful, and helped him prepare the messages he would send to the concerned people. Once the copy was as he wanted, he watched the telegrapher sit at his desk and with his finger on the telegraph key the man sent the message that read:

Sirs:
I regret to inform you that on the morning of May 5, 1856, at the Port of Rock Island, Illinois, a tragic accident occurred in which the steamer Effie Afton was destroyed, after hitting the piers of the railroad bridge. She caught fire, and it spread onto the bridge, causing loss of life, cargo and the complete destruction of the riverboat, Effie Afton. More details coming when available.

Remorsefully,
J.S. Hurd
Captain- Effie Afton

He was already planning how he would file suit against the railroad company for the loss of the steamer.

Once he had contacted all of them he turned his attention to finding the diver he knew who lived in this area. He remembered the man was a scrufty old man whose eyesight was very bad. Hurd thought it was kind of a funny a man half blind was an underwater diver. Yet, what difference did it make since under water it's almost impossible to see anything anyway.

It wasn't hard to find the old gent. Everyone in the area knew of him. He lived in a little old shack just west of Rock Island, in Kauke's Slough. His diving equipment included a rubber suit with a bronze diver's helmet that attached at the neck of the suit by way of a screw-on, ring-locking system. A skiff with a hand pump provided air to the diver when he was underwater. He had an assistant who provided the pumping action to get air to the diver.

The diver's name was Himmey Wolf, and his assistant was his son, Jeremy. Hurd made contact with him. They scheduled a time when he would come up to the place where the Afton was said to have disappeared and settled into a watery grave somewhere down river. Himmey was well versed in the mechanics of steamboats and all their equipment because he and his family did repairs and some construction of these kinds of boats. The diver wasn't too busy, and said he would get right on it.

Before he took the skiff to the scene, he spent some time with the Afton engine room mechanics to get as much information as he could about the mechanics and workings of the boat's steerage. What and how was it put together?

Once satisfied he had a good idea what he was looking for, he returned to the slough and started loading necessary tools and equipment onto the skiff. The skiff was driven by a small handbuilt steam engine which drove a paddlewheel at the stern, also handmade. The engine consisted of a steam boiler which was fueled by feeding wood onto a fire under it.
The steam engine turned a piston mechanism which turned the paddlewheel. The rudder was attached through the deck of the boat, and a steering-tiller was used to steer the

flat bottomed skiff. Because the rudder and tiller were ahead of the paddlewheel, it took constant effort to control the flatbottomed skiff. The skiff could be heard from a long way off as it puffed and paddled up to the site. Since Himmey's sight wasn't all that good, he would describe to the boy where he wanted to search for the wreckage, and the son would quickly point the skiff's bow toward the designated area. The day was much brighter today and the wind was much calmer making the assignment easier. When the boy told Himmey he was satisfied he was in the search area which Himmey wanted to drag for the wreckage, Himmey told the boy to stop the engine. The boy would now pole while Himmey would drag for something he felt might be a portion of the wreck.

They were a little upriver from where he believed the boat might have settled on the river bottom. Himmey wanted to use the current to their advantage. Several passes were made before he felt the gaff catch something he thought might be what they were looking for. Telling the boy to set the anchor, he started to get ready for a descent into the murky waters.

First, he pulled on a pair of heavy wool socks that came up over his knees and a pair of long cotton underwear. Then, once the anchor was holding, the boy unfolded the heavy, rubber diving suit, and made it ready for Himmey to slip his feet into the legs. The upper half was tougher to get into because of the metal ring he had to slip his head through. The metal ring was where the diving helmet attached and would seal itself to the suit.

A leaded belt sealed the two-piece suit and acted as ballast to keep the diver under water. The helmet was slipped over the diver's head and twisted onto the metal ring of the suit. Himmey then slipped into and buckled on a pair of heavy lead shoes that would keep him on the bottom of the river. Then a hose was attached to the helmet to provide air to the diver. Now the boy must start pumping the pump handle while the diver crawled over the side of the skiff. This was an enormous effort because of the heavy lead shoes.

As Himmey slid into the water, bubbles and gurgles rose out of the suit. He gently disappeared into the black murk.

Pumm shhhh, Pumm shhhh. Pumm shhhh. The pump pushed air down to the diver.

Feeling around as he walked along the bottom, Himmey suddenly felt something that wasn't naturally common to the river bottom.

"Yes! It could be the Afton," he thought.

As he moved more down river, he sensed it was the boat. He unfortunately was at the bow and would have to work his way back up river, fighting against the current where the engine and steering mechanism would be located. Feeling his way as he went, he recognized the broken and bent remains of the boat's structure that wasn't burned off or torn off the hull in its struggle against the forces of the bridge.

Moving cautiously toward the stern of the boat he found the passageway into the engine room. He had to force his way into the area by moving fallen timbers and debris in order to find the steering mechanism.

Once there, he began to feel parts that were described to him by the engine mechanics. He moved along the heavy rod linkage that attached the rudder assembly to the steering yoke. This yoke was what turned the rudder. It was directly above the rudder shaft. He felt the area where the parts met to complete the steering system.

"That's funny," he thought to himself as he slid his hand along the top of the heavy bronze yoke. "There's a bolt and nut on this side that connects the rudder shaft plate to the yoke plate, but as I move to the other side of the yoke plate the bolt that should be there is missing. It was meant to keep the two plates correctly positioned. I believe the linkage from the pilot's wheel could turn but couldn't necessarily turn the rudder. Looks like Captain Hurd's Effie Afton may have been sabotaged."

Continuing his search, he found on the deck below the rudder mechanism a large bolt that matched the one on the right side of the rudder yolk. Feeling with his cold bare hands he could tell that the bolt had been cut off because the nut was still attached. Yes, and here was the top part of the bolt also lying directly under the yoke on the engine room floor. Putting the two pieces into a pouch that was attached to his diving suit he started back to where his skiff was anchored.

He broke the surface by pulling himself up to the boat and onto a ladder that Jeremy positioned for him. He pulled himself up so his helper could twist the heavy helmet from its seat. Jeremy lifted the helmet into the skiff.
Himmey pulled himself up the ladder removing each lead boot one at a time and lowering them into the bottom of the boat. Then, taking off the heavy lead belt, he let it slide into the boat as he raised himself over the gunnel into a sitting position onto one of the boat benches.

Captain Hurd was waiting for him on shore as they glided into the slough and the bow of the skiff beached to a halt.

"Find anything?" the captain asked.

"Yes sir," Himmey replied as he pulled off the rest of the diving suit. "Your boat was probably sabotaged. Here's what I found."

He showed the captain the two pieces that had been a complete bolt. He had found them just below the rudder mechanism. "This bolt exactly matches the one on the other side of the rudder yolk and it wasn't where it should have been. It appears to have been cut off," he said.

Captain Hurd was taken aback and took the two pieces. He shook his head in amazement. "Who could have done this? Would it have prevented the pilot's control of the boat?" he stared at Himmey in disbelief.

"In my book, Sir, that's a definite possibility," Himmey

assured him.

May seventh saw the sun rise from the east in a brilliantly clear, cloudless sky. The sun was warming the entire surroundings. Spring was definitely showing her colors. The red buds were at their most vibrant purples and reds.

Philip was excited at the idea of Virginia's coming aboard and accompanying him on the trip through the rapids to LeClaire. There they'd leave the Carson, and join his family overnight, before their canoe trip down the rapids.

Virginia was right on time, bounding up the gangway carrying her bag. She was dressed in a long flowing skirt ballooned by several layers of petticoats and the sleeves of her blouse were flowing well beyond the form of her arms. She was wearing a large brimmed bonnet that identified her as being among the well-educated, well-bred young women of the day. She looked a little more daring than most of her contemporaries by the way she carried herself. It showed as she greeted every boatman along the way to the Carson bridge. A friendly touch and smile was directed to everyone. She was definitely going to have a good time. It showed, and no one saw it more apparently than Philip. He loved the way she demanded admiring gazes from everyone onboard. Captain Brickle gave Philip a wink of approval.

"Philip, what a nice day! Will we be able to get up through the bridge?" she asked.

"Ask the Captain," Philip retorted.

"The answer is *yes*," Brickle interjected.

"Philip, I'm so excited. It's going to be so much fun."

"Prepare to cast off," was Brickle's order to his deck crew. They began untying the mooring lines that held the steamer against the dockage. "You've got the helm," he waved to Philip.

The engines turned the large sidewheels as Philip instructed by use of the bell ropes that informed the engine room he was needing power. The J.B. Carson began to move away from the dock and turn her bow out into the river, and headed toward the bridge. The current had subsided and it wasn't necessary to use a lot of engine power to get the boat moving in the right direction. With whistles blowing, and smoke pouring from the large smokestacks, the J.B. Carson was announcing she was getting under way.

Virginia was totally engrossed in watching Philip at the wheel, piloting the boat toward the bridge and onto the fearsome rapids. How well he handled the large craft, spinning the large wheel to the desired course.

There were still several boats tied up at both the Rock Island and Davenport levees. Virginia watched intently as they pulled away from the docks, and as they maneuvered into the middle of the river. She liked the view from here. Everything seemed so sculptured, green and blue. A few scattered residences appeared high upon the bluffs over the growing city of Davenport. An occasional flock of ducks flew by the port side of the Carson, honking happily. She could see a muskrat scurrying for cover along the shoreline.

"There it is!" Philip pointed ahead to the open span of the new, burned bridge. To the right, that big pier in the center is where the Effie Afton first hit the bridge. It appears there is nothing there, that I can see, to be an obstruction to us. Anyway, we'll slow down and make our way up to it very cautiously."

With that, he pulled the bell rope, ordering the engine backed off on the throttle indicator. The tinkling of bells sounded, alerting the engine room that a change in speed was required. Virginia felt an easing of the forward motion and saw the bow rise up slightly. Philip adjusted the wheel several times in both directions to offset the tendency for the boat to fishtail. Once everything had settled down and less adjustments were required at the helm, the steamer was coming onto the gap of the bridge. Philip chose to enter on the starboard side of the large pier. He thought that side seemed to have less current and fewer eddies swirling around the structure. Everything seemed to be clear and he ordered a little more power as they entered the center of the span.

The Carson plowed into the rapidly moving water and easily passed the center of the span. He pointed out to Virginia a portion of the bridge that was badly damaged and burned. She nodded and said, "How awful! Can it be repaired?"

Philip assured her that it could be operating again in no time at all, "Probably will be rebuilt and in operation in less than a month."

"Really?" she seemed surprised at his quick response. "Father would be pleased if it could. He was concerned about how long it would be before it could be in operation again."

The stern of the Carson was almost in the clear of the gap, and Virginia had to look to the rear of the boat to study the overall length of the bridge, visualizing the revolving, swing portion completed and back in place. A spectacular site, to say the least, and what a great addition to the country when the trains could span the Mississippi into the West.

She recalled her father's telling her how many people were greatly opposed to the bridge at Rock Island-Davenport. He had said that because the free/slave controversy was rising so fast and becoming such an issue between the North and the South, each side wanted the first bridge over the Mississippi River to favor their personal interests.

"War must be inevitable!"

Philip broke her train of thought by pointing out several places of interest, such as where Chief Blackhawk and his Sauk Tribe had once camped along the river. He also told her that Lt. Robert E. Lee spent much of his early career surveying the river. Many people who now held important government positions had served in the Indian-American war, such as Secretary of War -Jefferson Davis. Virginia was impressed with Philip's knowledge of history.

"Now, on your right, do you see that rough-looking water? That's the beginning of the rapids."

The Carson would have no problem navigating through the rapids, but care must be taken to not be fooled by submerged rocks. They sometimes moved because of the current and became a menace.

"I am pretty familiar with this section but sometimes find things I am not expecting. Have to stay on my toes," Philip said as he guided the big boat up through the rapids. "It'll look a lot different when we come down in the birch canoe. You brought warm clothes, I hope. The water is still quite chilly."

She quickly responded. "I have some boy clothes I felt more appropriate for the trip in the canoe. They will be quite warm and not as conspicuous as a long dress and head covering we girls wear today. I can put my hair up in braids to make it easier to handle while canoeing. "It'll be so much fun."

"Well, it's hard work…I trust your canoe skills are up to it."

"My dear sir, I was on the girls' rowing team at school for four years. Even captain of my team my last year."

"OHH, I'm relieved. I thought I had a green horn," he said

with a grin as he maneuvered around a large boulder area with the white water thrashing around the large rocks. This truly was white water beyond her experience. She could see this would be an adventure. She loved it.

Captain Hurd received the messenger at his hotel in Rock Island, bringing a reply from his dispatched message. It was from T.D. Lincoln, the attorney from Cincinnati.
It read:

Sir:
Need more information, if you please. We could have a lawsuit to pursue. Proceed at all costs. Most important.

Signed,
T.D. Lincoln
Attorney at Law
Cincinnati, Ohio

"I must get the engineers together and see if we can establish the cause of the accident now that I have the diver's information which might indicate sabotage," Hurd said to himself.

He found some of his crew and told them of the plan to get all together and discuss the information he had concerning the rudder control. A room at the local hotel was chosen for the meeting. All but one was available and in attendance.

When they all settled down, Captain Hurd emptied a bag containing the two pieces of the bolt which the diver had

found on the wreck.
Hurd explained they had been cut. That, according to the diver, left one side of the rudder housing unattached.

Immediately, one of the engineers spoke up.

"Sir, I checked the rudder system that morning before we got underway and everything was intact."

Next James Parker, pilot of the Effie Afton rose and said, "Are you telling me that my suspicions are correct? I knew when we were wedged upon that big pier we had no control over the boat. I asked for reverse power to back away from the pier. Got the power, but could not get steerage to move away from it. At first I thought it was the current and the eddies forcing us onto the piling, but as I fought the wheel, I realized nothing was happening to help steer away from it. I've spent all night blaming myself for what has happened to the boat, the people and the cargo lost because of it. Maybe *that's* what that stranger was doing in the engine room when we were helping passengers with their equipment and cargo on the first deck."

Another piped up and said, "I thought I saw that guy later that night standing around with a bunch of protestors. They were all drinking and having a good ol' time."

"Could you identify him if you saw him again?"

"I think so. I remember he was wearing a bowler hat, and his coat and vest didn't match his knickers. He was carrying a bag that rattled when he moved it. Like something metal inside."

Hurd thought, stroking his chin and raising his hand as he picked up the bolt parts and said, "Let us find the bastard who did this--If anyone sees him let me know immediately. I'll let the authorities know so they can pick him up for questioning. I have already talked to the police so they know about the possible sabotage. According to a message I received from the attorney, we may have a suit to file against the railroad and bridge company."

Picking up the bolt parts, he walked to the door indicating the meeting was over, and as each man passed through the door he thanked them for coming.

10

CHAPTER TEN: GETTING ACQUAINTED IN LeCLAIRE

The river runs east and west until the end of the rapids and the river then turns north and immediately LeClaire, Iowa, comes into view... a sleepy little town spotted with several beautiful Victorian houses all facing the river. All were owned by prominent river pilots.

"That big one there with the big green and white veranda is the home of Captain Smith. He's the first sought after pilot here. Well into his eighties, but still knows every nook and cranny between here and Rock Island. Fought in two wars, wounded three times. I've learned a lot about the river from him. Walks with a cane given to him by a fella from Galena by the name Ulysses S. Grant.

Grant is presently retired but well thought of by everyone, despite the fact he has a drinking problem. I ran into Grant one day over at Maquoketa in a hotel bar. He'd been drinking rather heavily that day. Nice man even so. He seemed intent upon reentering the army."

"That gray house, just on the bluff there, is where my family lives. I stay with them when I'm here because it gives me someone to talk to other than the boys down at the hotel. See that big old tree there on the bank? That's the "Green Tree," so it's called. It's where the boats dock and pick up their pilots for going down river, and where those going north drop off the pilot who has brought them up through the rapids. We'll be docking in there shortly."

Philip pulled the bell rope and moved the throttle handle to the one-third position. The big boat slid to a creeping forward direction toward the docking facility. There were many people standing at the foot of the dock as some passengers were getting off there.

Philip could see his mother waving to him because he had sent word that he would probably arrive today and would have a visitor with him. She was elated because she was hoping that her son would find someone and settle down soon. He wasn't getting any younger, and she was looking forward to enjoying grandchildren she so wanted to have. She already had a homesite picked out for him less than three blocks away.

The big steamer slowed to a stop as it settled into the slip. After she was securely tied up, Philip was able to leave his post in the pilothouse. Captain Brickle was already exchanging pleasantries with Philip's mother, from his favorite spot along the deck rail.

"Come Virginia, let's go meet my mother." Philip instructed.

Leaving the pilot house and descending the two decks onto the main deck they scurried down the gangplank onto the dock where his mother was waiting.

"Mother, this is Virginia Sheffield, the girl I mentioned in my message." He interrupted the conversation his mother was having with Captain Brickle.

Brickle stepped aside and crossed his arms, giving his famous wink to the elder woman, insinuating this might be the one she was hoping for.

Jane Suiter, Philip's mother, was a true damsel of the river. She loved the freshness of it all. Seeing the spring flowers blooming, the birds nesting and returning to unfrozen waters, making new nests and filling them with offspring. Especially now when her son brought a lady to visit. That hadn't happened very often, even though he was in his early thirties. She was sorry that her husband wasn't here to help welcome Philip's friend.

Josh Suiter, Philip's father was still on a trip up to Saint Paul on the "Diamond Jo," another large steamboat carrying a large cargo and many passengers. He had been gone over a week. She assumed he was due back sometime before nightfall.

" I'm pleased to meet you, Virginia. How did you like the trip through the rapids?" she asked with interest.

"It was wonderful," Virginia assured her. " I can't wait to do the rapids with Philip in his canoe...
and I'm so very pleased to meet you," .

Jane Suiter thought to herself, "Well, this might be the one. Philip would have to find someone who would share his love for the river and nature. Even being on the risky, adventurous side, which she appears to be."

She ended her thought by saying, "Let's walk up to the house where we can visit. Josh might get here a little later. We'll wait a while before we have supper."

Philip nodded in agreement. "Is that okay with you Virginia?"

"Fine with me."

"Will the Carson be here overnight or will she continue up river? I'd like to ask Captain Brickle to join us if they will be docked here for the evening. "

"He'd love to, I'm sure, Mother, but he's anxious to get up to Dubuque with some cargo and passengers he is concerned about. There is a young woman and her daugther who were passengers aboard the Effie Afton when it hit and set fire to the railroad bridge and sank. We were able to save her, but all her belongings were lost. Brickle was able to find enough clothes for her and her daugther while they are enroute to Dubuque. Her husband is waiting for their arrival. He has work in Galena where they plan to make their residence."

"Very well then, let me tell him goodbye."

The three walked over to the boat where Captain Brickle came to meet them. They said their goodbyes, shook hands and as they were parting, Brickle said to Virginia, "You take care and don't let that boy drown on that canoe trip through the rapids. I'll be needing him, you know."

"Rest assured, and have a good trip," she jibed.

The three walked toward the road that led up to the Suiter home. Half way up the hill they heard the long horn blasts from the J.B. Carson indicating she had steam up and was about to get underway. All three turned back toward the dock to watch the Carson. They paused momentarily to watch the big steamer pull away from its mooring.

The walk was less than a quarter of a mile before they arrived at the house. It was a typical Victorian design with large square columns supporting the veranda. Virginia could feel its hospitality and warmth even before she stepped onto the long expansive porch. Large white wicker rocking chairs were stategically placed on the porch that offered a wonderful view of the river.

Jane Suiter moved in front of the two younger people and opened the door into the vestibule.

"Welcome to our home," she invited.

They all three entered and she suggested they go into the living room. The next four hours were spent with Jane becoming better acquainted with Virginia.

Jane Suiter delighted in showing Virginia around the big house, stopping here and there to pick up a photograph or a memento of her son that showed him at different ages and in many of his activities. Philip was embarrassed and begged her not to make him the subject of her tour.

It was about seven o'clock when they heard the toot, toot of the "Diamond Jo" as she had already had steamed through Steamboat Slough. Steamboat Slough was only about five miles from LeClaire.

Jane said, "Josh will be here soon, I'd better get supper ready." Philip wondered whether the word "supper" seemed as Midwestern to Virginia as "dinner" was Eastern to him.

Philip's mother disappeared into the kitchen. Philip invited Virginia to join him on the veranda to see the "Diamond Jo" steaming by into LeClaire.

They walked to the edge of the veranda and saw the "Diamond Jo" come into view. It was becoming dusk and as the sun settled into the western horizon, the last light painted the eastern Illinois shoreline with a brilliant white glow. The shoreline was dotted with trees and a few scattered houses now visible across the Mississippi. The geese and migrating ducks scattered on the water shone like stars with the last light of day.

Virginia took Philip's arm in hers and said, "Philip, this is a wonderful place. I can see why you love it so much."

The "Diamond Jo" slipped easily into the LeClaire dock. The crew made ready all her lines and completed all her docking requirements.

When the boat was securely docked, Josh Suiter bounded down the gangplank, patting members of the crew on their arms. Josh was a little surprised that Jane wasn't at the dock to greet him. But, she often got busy and didn't always know when he'd be returning.

Josh Suiter, having finished all his duties aboard the "Diamond Jo," including his paper requirements, then set about leaving the boat to hurry home to his wife, Jane. It would be a well deserved rest from the many days on the river. Anyway, he'd just hustle up the hill to the house. Hopefully, she'd have supper ready, guessing he'd be home tonight.

Entering the house and calling for his wife, Philip interceded saying, "Father, you're home...Mother and I have a surprise visitor. This is Virginia Sheffield."

Virginia was surprised to see the resemblance between father and son. The father, however, due to his years, was slightly heavier. An image of Virginia's grandfather rushed through her head. He, when comparing two people related to each other having similar appearances, always made the comment that "the apple doesn't fall far from the tree." He would then chuckle as if he'd said something really profound.

Collecting her thoughts, she held out her hand conveniently for Josh Suiter to bring the back of her hand to his lips. He looked directly into her eyes and said, "I'm delighted to meet you, my dear. Please just call me Josh," the river pilot proposed.

"Father, I met Virginia several weeks ago in Rock Island. We were together two days ago, after the railroad bridge disaster. Have you heard about the Effie Afton setting fire to the bridge and then sinking in a firey pyre?"

"Yes, the news has alreay traveled up and down the river," he answered.

Virginia acknowledged the introduction, and proceded to join Philip's mother in the kitchen to see if there was anything she could do to help.

Josh pulled Philip aside and asked, " Philip, what's going on here? Who is this girl?"

"Her father is an executive of the Rock Island & Chicago Railroad Co. As I said, I met Virginia while I was there on several different occasions while on piloting assignments. We became friends, and she has stated an interest in doing the rapids with me in my birch canoe starting from here at LeClaire."

" My God, does she have all her faculties?" his father asked kiddingly.

"Of course," Philip responded. "I'll admit she's a little different. Brought clothes to dress like a boy when we go through the rapids. Doesn't seem to have any fear of them at all…"

"Where's she from?" Josh asked.

"Out East. She has a law degree from Yale. She came here to live with her father in the absence of her deceased mother."

"She's a lawyer? There aren't many women lawyers around here," Josh mused.

Then changing the subject, Josh continued, "Yes, upriver, we heard about the Effie Afton disaster at Rock Island. Some were saying it was a problem created by the currents that persist around the new railroad bridge piers. Others say that one of the big sidewheels stopped working and Parker, the pilot, couldn't control the boat. Some say that the railroad and bridge will be sued by the boat people, headed by the owners of the Effie Afton. One of them is Captain Hurd, as I recall." I've piloted for him. Seemed very nice," Josh remembered.

"Supper is served," announced Jane Suiter.

Philip attended the chair for Virginia, then for his mother. He then seated himself next to Virginia. His father took his place as usual at the head of the table.

Looking at Virginia, he said, "Shall we give thanks to the Lord for our blessings?"

Automatically, Virginia bowed her head waiting for him to begin the prayer, giving a little peak from one corner of her eye at Philip to see whether or not she was doing everything right. He gave her a glancing look of approval.

Josh always enjoyed testing strangers at "supper." He was always interested to see how his guests responded to suppertime prayer, and Virginia had passed the test. Here at the Suiter home, a time for thanks was always celebrated at the evening meal and always given by the head of the house. Josh began,

" Thanks be to God.
We ask your blessings on this home
and for those who have joined us this evening..
Bless this food we are about to receive,
that it will nourish our bodies.
Bless those who have gone on before us.
Give us peace in the land.
We ask it all in the name of the Son. Amen."

Josh then began passing a large bowl of white fluffy mashed potatoes even before all heads were raised. Next, he offered a large platter of fried chicken accompanied by vegetables consisting of fresh carrots, and steamed zuccini. It was a wonderful meal, topped off with pie with her own canned peaches.

11

CHAPTER ELEVEN: SHOOTING THE RAPIDS

Virginia was awakened early hearing the lovely sound of birds coming from a wooded area behind the LeClaire house. A rooster was announcing the sun was coming up over the river through a small layer of clouds emitting red, orange and yellow rays, burning off the haze as it rose in the east.

She liked it here. She could see the famous "Green Tree" from the window in the guest room she had been assigned. Philip said it was a landmark for every river man. The tree was not tall but had the shape of an immense mushroom. She had laid out the clothes she would wear for the adventure down the river through the rapids the night before. She was a little nervous, but anxious to get going.

"It should be a great time," she thought. She hoped her experience from school in the rowing club would be helpful. She didn't want to be a burden to Philip. "He is such a dear to take me through the rapids in the canoe."

Philip leaving his room and greeting Virginia in the hallway, took her hand and asked, "Did you sleep well?"

"Oh yes, soundly. It's a beautiful day for a boat ride," trying to hide her anxiety. Those white caps she saw were a little more intense than she had imagined. Philip said he wanted to go over a few things with her about the trip after they had eaten breakfast.

Jane Suiter was up and about in the kitchen fixing their breakfast and preparing food for the trip as she had done so many times for Philip.

"Good morning, my dear, are you ready for the rapids?" she greeted Virginia noticing the unlady like dress that Virginia had chosen for the day trip.

"I think so."

Breakfast finished, Virginia and Philip said their goodbyes as Josh suddenly appeared. He liked sleeping later after working all week, but wanted to see the two off on the trip through the rapids.

Philip kept the canoe down by the river in a shelter, along with paddles, life preservers and some things he felt necessary to have along, in case; items such as dry protected matches, and emergency medical kit, wool clothing including stocking hats. There would be a place to stop off, rest, enjoy the sandwiches, cookies and fruit prepared for them by his mother.

Philip turned the canoe over. Virginia could see the three seats, bow and stern with a larger seat in the middle. Philip was busy tying extra paddles to the middle seat and handing one to Virginia, keeping one for himself. Everthing else was put into a hammock sling and tied securely to the middle seat.

Virginia asked, "Why so many paddles?

"Just in case we lose one," Philip assured her. "You've heard the expression, (*Up a river without a paddle.*)

"No, that's a new one."

Philip finally looked up at her, and said they were about ready to put the canoe in the water. It would slide in easily. He held and steadied the boat while Virginia climbed aboard.

Once in and seated she noticed the current rushing by under the boat. Philip then stepped into the stern of the canoe as he pushed the bow away from the shore.

Once moving in the current downstream, a mallard hen and her four ducklings scurried out of the way. The mother duck paddled noisily and scolded the canoeists for distrubing her babies' training session. Virginia looked back up the hill toward the Suiter house and saw Philip's parents waving. She also noticed several fishermen watching as they passed by. The river was starting its bend toward the west and she was beginning to see the dark water ahead...the rapids.

Philip had instructed if the canoe turned over and threw them into the water, she was to stay with the canoe. The canoe would not sink. It could be easily righted and carefully gotten aboard. You will be wet but with only hurt feelings," he assured her.

The water was becoming more rapid. They were beginning to feel the rush from the speeding current. Philip did most of the steering from the back and Virginia kept the bow pointed where Philip was steering. Now the bow was beginning to crash into the waves, sometimes diving and sending sprays of water over the bow.

It became more fun and more intense as they got deeper into the swirling rapids. Sometimes Virginia even felt herself leave the seat as the boat dropped suddenly from under her as they crashed through powerful waves.

"What a thrill this is," she yelled at Philip.

He smiled and stroked his paddle forcefully to steer them

through the rough white water, missing boulders that appeared and disappeared as they paddled and dived into the waves. Philip had chosen to stay more on the outer edge of the channel so Virginia could get the full effect of the rapids.

About halfway through the course, Philip announced that they would put in at an island called "Campbell's Island," rest and have lunch. Virginia thought it a good idea as she was getting a little tired from the pounding and the use of her arms. She could tell it was hard work for Philip as the current was so powerful. To steer through the rapids required real technical knowledge as well as muscle power. However, she was enjoying it so much.

"We are passing the wildest part of the rapids," Philip announced as he started to steer toward Campbell's Island.

It was a welcome break, and the island was lush and well inhabited with wildlife.

The two enjoyed their leisurely lunch and rested for some time just reviewing the highpoints of the trip so far.

While they rested lounging on the ground in the swaying prairie grasses, Philip pointed to a far end of the island and said, "Virginia, see that point that sticks out over there? Once when I was alone doing the rapids I capsized and had to swim with the canoe ashore over there to get myself put back together and dry off. I had just wrung out my clothes and things and had hung them on bushes to dry. Suddenly a young uniformed man rode up to me on horseback leading a mule with saddle bags hanging on both flanks of the animal full of surveying equipment. I was surprised to see him here in the wilderness, but recognized him as an army officer. His name was Lieutenant Robert E. Lee. He was surveying and mapping this part of the Mississippi River."

Philip also showed Virginia where a part of the Blackhawk war had occured on the island. He also pointed out where the great warrior Blackhawk was captured. Virginia was overly impressed with the history lesson.

By now the sun was high in the sky and Philip thought it would be a good idea if they packed up and got started again. There were still plenty of rapids to navigate.

Back in the canoe and crashing down an alley of boulders, you could hear them laugh and scream up into the hills on both sides of the river. Cautiously, they made their way down river through the Rock Island rapids toward the city of Rock Island.

CHAPTER TWELVE: THE WRIT HAS BEEN FILED

Captain Hurd opened the door of his hotel room, and admitted the messenger who had been dispatched with the answer from the lawyer in Cincinnati. Evidently, some of the owners had gotten together and discussed the situation. They were unanimous in recommending an immediate filing of a lawsuit against the railroad company to try to recover the loss of the Effie Afton. The message stated that a committee was enroute to Rock Island, where they felt it would be more favorable to conduct the preparations, find witnesses and view the area where the accident had occurred. Hurd was happy that he had received such a quick response to his last message from the lawyer. He also agreed that setting up operations here in Rock Island seemed appropriate to him. Now he felt as if he weren't carrying the load all by himself.

He suddenly realized he had not eaten since earlier this morning. Now, with some of the relief that had come from this new message, he was suddenly hungry. "Why not go and get something to eat?" he asked himself. "There must be a good cafe around here someplace. I'll ask at the desk."

The clerk at the counter directed him to the cafe just around the corner called Dickson's Cafe. Entering, he was shown to a nice table by a very pleasent young lady who worked as a waitress.

The facility was clean and tidy. He ordered a turkey dinner, and was happy with the service and the food.

He overheard three fellows sitting across the room from him saying they had heard there was a big protest rally against the bridge being planned for that night.

A silver dollar covered his bill and a gratuity for his waitress.
As Captain Hurd was leaving the cafe, he noticed a lot of activity down the street. He walked toward the area and saw some people waving banners and getting very excited about something. The commotion seemed to be coming

from the residential area of the town.
Hurd thought he'd stick around to see what was happening.

Following at a safe distance behind the small group of protestors, he could see they meant business. The boats at the landing were starting to blow their whistles, sometimes in unison. Some were just large annoying blasts, and some were like dinner bells.

Hurd continued to get closer and noticed the group gathering in front of a large residence. They were well organized, and becoming violent. What they were up to he didn't know, but it appeared that they were up to no good.

They made their way toward this large home with an iron fence around its perimeter. The iron gate featured an "S" emblazoned on it. Two of the men unloaded a large bag of wood in front of the gate, teepeeing it into a tall tent-like fashion, and poured some kind of fluid onto it. Then, stepping back, they made way for a large, mean-looking character to move up to the pile of wood and throw a lighted, rag- wrapped stick onto the pile. A large flash and a flame rose up twelve feet or so.

Kaaboom!
There was a frightening sound when it ignited. Then suddenly the door to the house flew open and a man appeared holding a shotgun in his hands.

"Whats going on here?" he demanded.

The leader answered, "You're one of the people respon-

sible for that damn bridge, aren't you?"
Before there was time for any answers, the police had arrived on the scene, and had two of the men under arrest. The big man had taken off running with three of the policemen hot on his heels screaming. "Halt...Halt...in the name of the law."

The big guy just kept running. The officers must have known who the man was and they kept yelling. "Stop, or we'll shoot." The man just kept going.

Two shots rang out and Hurd saw the man go down on his knees, and then fall over onto his stomach.

By now the crowd began to dissipate. When one of the officers walked by, Hurd asked him who the man was.

The officer told him it was Joe Piaza. "Someone we've been looking for for sometime. He's wanted for many things up and down the river. He's even wanted for murder."

Even though Hurd agreed with some of the protestors' frustrations, he didn't want to become involved in the violence that seemed to be much of what this demonstration was all about. Now someone was wanted for murder.

"No, sir. I'll do my protesting in a court of law." Besides, he now had some concern that there was sabotage aboard his boat that may have borne some of the responsibility for hitting the bridge.
If that were the case, the only argument concerning the bridge was that it was a hazard to navigation.

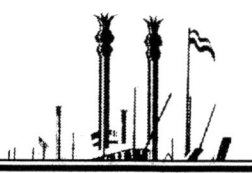

CHAPTER THIRTEEN: THE SPRINGFIELD LAWYER APPEARS AT THE BRIDGE

Abe Lincoln had received a call from Norman B. Judd, the General Counsel for the Rock Island Railroad, and one of the Bloomington convention organizers of the Republican party, requesting that Mr. A. Lincoln represent the company. He was instructed to contact Mr. Sheffield, a director of the railroad company, who had overseen completion of the bridge. He was asked to represent them if a suit were filed against them by the Effie Afton owners and the representatives of the boating people who felt the bridge was a obstacle to safe navigation on the river. They feared that if this bridge were allowed to stand, then many others would soon appear up and down the river.

Mr. Lincoln had made the trip from Springfield, Illinois, by carriage to Rock Island. It had been a long, grueling trip. He had insisted on seeing the bridge immediately upon his arrival into the Rock Island area. Brushing off the road dust, he untangled his long lanky legs and righted himself onto the surface below the carriage door. Looking around and surveying the surroundings, he immediately focused on the bridge before him. Seeing the bridge first hand would give Mr. Lincoln some thoughts from which he could map out an approach to his work on the next day.

He noticed a small boy standing on the bridge who was throwing scraps of wood that were remains of the bridge fire and walked toward him. The boy was throwing the sticks into the current and watching the current carry them around the pier. Upon seeing the man approaching, the boy stopped his throwing into the water.

Mr. Lincoln saw something about the way the boy's sticks would get caught in the eddys and swirl around the pier without hitting it.

"Does it do that every time when you throw the sticks into the water?" he asked.

"Yes, sir!" the boy assured him.

"What's your name?"

"Ben Brayton, Jr. " The boy said proudly.

"I'm eleven years old. I live here in Rock Island. My Father is the chief engineer for the railroad company...he built the railroad bridge and now hes going to rebuild it."

Lincoln smiled at the boy's convincing attitude.

"Why do you think the sticks always miss running into the pier?"
"They never do," the boy answered.
"The current swirls around the pier and the stick is sort of caught up into the eddy and is swished away from the stationary pylon."

"Very interesting, Benjamin." He walked around in the vicinity and took in every angle he could find from this spot. He seemed intrigued by the whole situation, at which time Mr. Sheffield came strolling up to him.

"Mr. Lincoln?" he asked.

"Yes, I'm Abe Lincoln." He extended his hand to the man.

Mr. Sheffield put his hand on Mr. Lincoln's arm, shook his hand and said, "You're probably hungry after your trip. My daughter is away until later today, but would love to meet you. She should be home soon. She's a recent law graduate from Yale."

"She has met and become friends with a river pilot. They went to LeClaire, Iowa, last night in order to run the rapids in a canoe.

She should be back sometime this evening."

"Interesting, I would love to visit with her and the river pilot, too. We might have need for someone of her legal background when we get into this case."

Virginia and Philip paddled exhausted into the Rock Island levee. They had taken their time on the last leg of their trip. Philip pulled the canoe up onto a safe place.

Virginia insisted that they go to her home so she could change into clothes more befitting a young lady of class. Philip had brought a change of clothes with him. Both were dragging their feet.

Arriving at the house they noticed the charred remains of a small wood fire. "What's this all about?" she exclaimed as she hurried to the door. The maid greeted her, and explained the reason for what could have been a bad scene had not the police shown up in time. "Your father's okay and has gone to meet a gentleman arriving from Springfield by carriage."

"Thank God, I worry so about him."

Virginia showed Philip to a room where he could clean up. She went upstairs to change and get out of those "wet boy clothes".

Mr. Seffield and his guest arrived shortly after Philip and Virginia were changed and resting in the parlor. Asking them how the trip was, he didn't need an answer. He could see the pleasure written all over his daugther's face.

Philip answered, "Your daugther was great during the rapids ordeal."

Mr. Sheffield turned to Mr. Lincoln, and introduced to him his daughter and friend.

Mr. Lincoln, with his ability to remember faces and detail said, "It's my pleasure to meet you, Virginia. I believe if I'm not mistaken, I've had the pleasure of meeting this gentleman before. I believe it was at New Boston on the dock."

"That's correct," Philip related.

They all discussed the day's events with Lincoln, asking pointed questions concerning the Afton affair.

"If we go to trial, I must have witnesses who are expert rivermen. And I will be needing someone with a law background to do research. I believe you two fit the bill. Do we have a deal?"

Both agreed readily.

"Good! We'll start immediately as we will probably go to trial in a few months. It'll be a good fight, too, because there is so much at stake- not just for the railroad, or the boat people, but for the entire nation."

The cook announced dinner and everyone was happy and

excited about what was ahead.

The doctors had removed the bullet from "Big Joe's" side and this time all agreed he'd be able to stand trial.

Months passed and Virginia busied herself with the details of trial preparation. Philip, in between assignments on the river with the big boats, made himself available to Lincoln as a technical witness, and found a way to visit Virginia as often as possible.

Philip and Virginia found they loved doing things together, including many more canoe trips through the rapids. Virginia had mastered the rowing technique to Philip's approval. She was still trying to educate the protestors and had made some progress.

Philip's mother couldn't stop asking Philip if the relationship with Virginia was getting serious.

His only answer was, "Yes."

Months rolled by far too quickly and summer turned to an Indian fall.

CHAPTER FOURTEEN: THE TRIAL BEGINS IN CHICAGO

The preparation for Lincoln's argument to defend the bridge was plainly the call of all the old romance of the Mississippi River. The attorney would begin by pointing out that Saint Louis might wish that the Rock Island bridge should not stand, that with the bridge gone a larger volume of Iowa products would have to be shipped by way of Saint Louis. Meetings held in Saint Louis so indicated this fact. He pointed to the great channel of the Mississippi "flowing from where it never freezes to where it never thaws."

"However, there are many months when the upper Mississippi is not navigable. The current of travel has its rights east and west as well as north and south. The proper mode for all parties is to "live and let live." This bridge must be treated with respect in this court, and is not to be kicked about with contempt."

The trial was set for September of eighteen hundred and fifty-seven in Chicago. The Saloon Building was to be the site of the Federal District Court for the Northern District of Illinois.

The lawsuit was known legally as Hurd vs. The Rock Island Bridge Company, but more popularly was labeled the Effie Afton case. The Saloon courtroom occupied no more than forty square feet. The usual division for the judges, clerks and attorneys occupied perhaps twenty feet on the farther side with the usual courtroom furniture.

The rest of the room contained large benches for the accommodation of the public. A large stove of the box pattern was near the door. Dominating the entire scene, was the figure of Lincoln, even though Judd was technically Chief Council for the defense.

Virginia kept very busy doing research for Mr. Lincoln, finding witnesses and helping prepare for depositions. Philip spent a good deal of time answering questions concerning navigating the river. He was to be one of Lincoln's technical witnesses.

Lincoln went about studying everything he could find concerning measurements of the bridge. (Specifically the piers and how they affected the water, the currents, the eddies.) He pondered more than the technicality of the river, but specifically how the bridge and railroad would effect the entire country. There was growing travel from east to west that had to be considered. It was as important as the Mississippi traffic. It was growing larger and larger, with a rapidity never before seen in the history of the world.

In his own memory, Lincoln had seen Illinois grow from almost empty spaces to a population of a million and a half. There were Iowa and many other rising communities spreading into the Northwest. He recalled that during the time until the bridge disaster, the railroads had hauled 12,586 freight cars and 74,179 passengers. This was during the months when the river was frozen and could not be navigated. Yes, the bridge and the railroad operated year round.

"This bridge must be treated with respect in this court and not be kicked about with contempt. This current mode of travel has its right as well as that of the north and south," Lincoln theorized as he pounded his fist into his palm. He must try to convince the jury this was the most important consideration.

He would ask if the products of boundless, fertile country lying west of the Mississippi must, for all time, be forced to stop on its western bank, be unloaded from the cars, then loaded onto a boat; and after passage across the river, be reloaded onto cars on the other side.

"Civilization in the region to the west is definitely at issue. The main drive of my argument will be that one man has as good a right to cross a river as another has to sail up and down it." Lincoln seemed pleased at this conclusion.

He had more than enough technical information, knowing the angles of the piers, the curve of the river, the depth of the channel, the velocity of the current.

The "Saloon Building" was located at the southeast corner of Clark and Lake streets in Chicago. Judge McLean was to preside. Engineers, pilots, boat owners, river men, bridge builders were to attend. Some were to be called as witnesses. The case of the owners of the Effie Afton vs. the bridge company for damages was in session.

Norman B. Judd, General Council of the Rock Island Railroad was the person who called upon Abraham Lincoln to represent the company at the hearings. Another more distinguished attorney than A. Lincoln, was among Captain Hurd's council. He was from Cincinnati. Another Lincoln, T.D. Not related to A. Lincoln.

The case came to trial in September of 1857. It was a trial that not only the valley but the whole nation would watch with intense interest. Newspapers in Saint Louis and New Orleans sent special correspondents to cover it.

Very early, with the selection of a jury, it was plain that intense sectional interests were involved. Many jurors frankly admitted to sectional prejudice, and several said that their businesses would be hurt if the bridge were declared a nuisance. The delegation from Saint Louis and the other river towns heard this with anxiety. Chicago hardly seemed the place for such a trial.

The opening statement for Captain Hurd was made by H.M. Weed of Peoria. The prosecution would show that the railroad had deliberately placed the great pier in such a way as to create an obstruction to navigation. It was not that they opposed all bridges. They wanted no war on bridges.

"We do not say, Weed added, "that a bridge may not be built at Rock Island which will accommodate the wants of the railroad and the wants of river navigation also."

N.B. Judd, in his opening statement for the defense, claimed that they could prove that the Effie Afton was racing for the draw with the J.B. Carson.. The railroad charged the steamboat captain with being bribed to run his vessel against the bridge, thus making a case of obstructed navigation. The accusation, was of course, angrily denied. But when the bridge was accidentally burned, all the river craft gathered at the spot and let their whistles loose in sheer joy at the disaster.

Under these circumstances it required a cool head and an even temper to carry the day, and Lincoln was to equal the occasion.

"They were only insured against fire that effected the Effie Afton and excluded any other property."
"We say," Mr. Judd thundered out to the crowded courtroom, "that the river people purposely caused the accident and the fire to prove that the bridge was an obstruction to navigation. There would be no insurance to cover the lost bridge.

"The other side would like to believe that it is utterly impossible for any man not an idiot to note the disasters at Rock Island, and honestly ascribe them to any other cause than the huge obstruction to navigation which the Bridge Company have built there and insist shall remain. Even though lives by the score and property by the millions will be destroyed every year...We have rarely seen such illustration of supercilious insolence, as we have been presented by advocates of the bridge." He finished, bowing to the jury, turning and sending a glaring stare directly at Captain Hurd and Attorney T. Lincoln.

J.S. Hurd cringed, and eased back into the chair he occupied with his counsel.

CHAPTER FIFTEEN: LINCOLN STATES HIS CASE

The defense began its arguments.

After the usual recognition of the judge and jury, Abe Lincoln turned to the jury.

"It is foreign to my purpose to pursue or assail anybody, and although I may seem to grow earnest, I shall try not to be offensive or ill-natured. There is some conflict of testimony in this case, but one quarter of such a number of witnesses seldom agree, and even if all were on one side some discrepancy might still be expected. We are to try to reconcile them and to believe that they are not intentionally erroneous, as long as we can."

At this point in his argument Lincoln evidently fell back on his knowledge and the experience he had gained when he floated down the Mississippi on a flatboat to New Orleans with John Hanks a quarter of a century before.

" I will not speak of the angular position of the piers. What is the amount of the angle? The course of the river is a curve, and the pier is straight. If a line is produced from the upper end of the long pier straight with the pier to a distance of three hundred and fifty feet, and a line is drawn from a point in the channel opposite this point to the head of the pier, Colonel Nelson, one of the bridge architects, says they will form an angle of twenty degrees. But the angle, if measured at the pier, is seven degrees to make it exactly straight with the current. Would that make the navigation better or worse?"

"The witnesses of the plaintiff seem to think it was only necessary to say that the pier formed an angle with the current, and that settled the matter. Our more careful and accurate witnessess say that though they had been accustomed to seeing piers placed straight with the current, they could see that here the current had been made straight by us in having made this slight angle; that the water now runs just right; that it is straight and cannot be improved. They think that if the pier were changed, the eddy would be divided and the navigation improved.

"I am not now going to discuss the question of what is

material obstruction. We do not greatly differ about the law. "

The cases produced here are, I suppose, proper to be taken into consideration by the court in instructing a jury. Some of them, I think, are not exactly in point, but I am still willing to trust His Honor, Judge McLean, and take his instruction as law. What is reasonable skill and care? This is a thing of which the jury are to judge."

"I differ from the other side when it says that the riverboats are bound to exercise no more care than was taken before the building of the bridge. If we are allowed by the legislature to build the bridge, which will require them to do more than before, when a pilot comes along it is unreasonable for him to dash on, heedless of this structure which has been legally put there."

"The Afton came there on the 5th, and lay at Rock Island until next morning. When a boat lies up, the pilot has a holiday. The Effie Afton pilot, Captain Parker could have then gone to the bridge and gotten acquainted with the structure. Pilot Parker of the Effie Afton has shown here that he does not understand the draw, and didn't take the time to review the new structure. I heard him say that the fall from the head to the foot of the pier was four feet. He needed more information; he could have merely taken time to go to the bridge, studied the piers and the eddies, and the chances are that he would have had no disaster at all. As a professional river pilot, he was bound to make himself acquainted with the place.

Two technical witnesses for the plaintiff both say the currents around the piers caused the Afton to crash into the piers. The first to testify, Mr. McCammon, an authority on river currents, says that the current and the swell coming from the long pier drove the Afton against the long pier; in other words, drove her toward the very pier from which the current came!"

"It is an absurdity--an impossibility. The only explanation I can find for this contradiction is in a current which the second river authority to testify, was Mr. White who says the currents strikes out from the long pier, and then like a ram's horn turns back. If this were true the current might have acted somehow in the manner describe by Parker."

"It is agreed by all that the plaintiff's boat was destroyed upon hitting the head of the short pier; then she moved from the channel with her bow above the head of the long pier till she again struck the short one and swung around under the bridge, pinned and destroyed." Lincoln pounds his fist in his hand, takes a deep breath and turns to the jury and begins again.

"I shall try to prove that the average velocity of the current through the draw with the boat in it should be five and a half miles an hour. The plaintiff's highest average is twelve miles an hour. Their testimony was made by men who made no experiment, only conjecture. Our argument consists of testimony using the most exact means and the most elaborate instruments."

"The water runs swiftest in high water so we have taken the point of nine feet above low water. The water when the Afton was lost was seven feet above low water or at least a foot lower than our number."

"Mr. Brayton and his assistant timed the instruments to check their accuracy. These were the best instruments for measuring currents. They timed the currents and eddies around the bridge piers and they found the current five miles and no more. They also found that the water at the upper end of the piers ran slower than five miles; but below it was swifter than five miles; but the average was five miles."

"Shall men who have taken no care, who conjecture, some of whom speak of twenty miles an hour, be believed against those who have employed the most scientific methods for measuring currents?" Mr. Abe Lincoln demanded.

"They would not even qualify the result." Lincoln said shaking his head.

"Several men have given their opinion as to the distance of the steamboat Carson was from the Afton at the time of the disaster.
I suppose if one should go and measure that distance, you would believe him in preference to someone making an opinionated judgement Their guesses were made when the boat was not in the draw. So what is truth? And how much can we believe without accurate measurements."

The distance of the cross section of the river going through the bridge and the area of the face of the piers has been ascertained. The engineers say that where the piers are placed in the river can increase the current proportionately, as the river's space is decreased because of the piers."

"So with the boat in the draw. The depth of the channel was twenty-two feet, the width one hundred and sixteen feet; multiply these and you have the square feet across the water of the draw. Two-thousand five-hundred and fifty-two feet if my arithmetic is correct." he says with both hand extended waiting for all to areee.

"The Afton was thirty-five feet wide and drew five feet, making a fourteenth of the sum. Now, one fourteenth of five miles is five-fourteenths of one mile--about one third of a mile--the increase of the current because of the space occupied by the Afton."

"We will call the current five and a half miles per hour. The next thing I will try to prove is that the plaintiff's boat had power to easily run six miles an hour in five and a half mile an hour in that current. It has been testified that the Effie Afton was a strong, swift boat able to run eight miles an hour upstream in a current of four miles an hour, and fifteen miles an hour downstream. Strike the average and you will find what is her average--about eleven and a half miles an hour."

"Take the five and a half miles, which is the speed of the current in the draw, and it leaves the power of that boat in that draw at six miles an hour or five hundred and twenty-eight feet per minute. The Afton should have cleared the draw of the bridge in only a few seconds."

"Next, I propose to show that there are no cross-currents. I know their witnesses say that there are cross-currents; that, as one witness says, there were three cross-currents and two eddies. This statement, made without experiment and mingled with mistakes... how can they make such absurb statements? But can these men's testimony be compared with the nice, exact and thorough experiments of our witnesses? Can you believe that these floats go across currents? It is inconceivable that they could. How do boats find currents that floating debris cannot discover? We assume the position, then, that those cross-currents do not exist."

"My next proposition is that the Afton passed between the J.B. Carson and the Iowa shore. That is undisputed. Based on where the Carson was when the Afton passed her, the Afton's course to the bridge was not a direct line into the draw."

"Next I shall show that she struck first the short pier, then the long pier, then the short one again, and there she stopped. How did the boat strike when she went in? Here is an endless variety of opinions--the testimony of eighteen witnesses."

But ten of them say what pier she struck; three of them testify that she struck first the short, then the long, and then the short for the last time. None of the rest substantially contradicted this... I assume that these men have the truth because I believe it is an established fact.

My next proposition is that after she struck the short and long pier and before she got back to the short pier, the boat got right with her bow up. So says the pilot Parker, that he got her through until her starboard wheel passed the short pier." This would make her head about even with the head of the longer pier. He says her head was as high or higher than that of the head of the long pier. Other witnesses confirmed this. The final impact was in the splash door aft one of the side wheels. Witnesses differ but the majority say that when she struck the long pier, she was sideways to the current."

"Could it be the pilot's inability or was there some mechanical problem that threw her at angle not in line with the current? Other witnesses show that the captain had said something of the machinery of the wheel or rudder, and the inference is that he knew the starboard wheel was not working. The pilot says he ordered the engineers to back her up. The engineers differ from him and said they kept on going ahead. The bow was so swung that the current pressed it over. The pilot tried to bring the stern over with the rudder. But with only one wheel in motion, the boat nearly stood still, with no response from the rudder, Thus she was thrown upon this pier."

At this point Lincoln paused and the court was adjourned, until the following day,

Lincoln resumed his argument, assuring the court that he would conclude as soon as possible.

Abe Lincoln had made himself so familiar with the figures, measurements, distances and facts in the case, that sometimes there was laughter as he rambled around the room looking abstracted, occasionally turning suddenly to correct a witness on a matter of feet or inches or the span of a truss. Especially vulnerable were witnesses trying to prove points regarding navigation. Lincoln not only spent hours walking the bridge, but a large boat was commissioned to make many trips up, down and through the bridge with Philip Suiter at the helm pointing out characteristics which involved boat handling in this kind of water.

After making objections, Lincoln would sit down by a big box stove, surrounded with cuspidors, and whittle, seemingly lost to the world. An instant came when he straightened up, walked toward a witness, and demanded that original notes as to certain measurements be produced. The witness was shown to be mistaken; it had its affect on the jury, and Lincoln went back to whittling by the big box stove.

With a whimsical sarcasm, he touched on the testimony that the boat had "smelled a bar," remarking, "For several days we were entertained with depositions about boats "smelling a bar."

"Why, then, did the Afton, after she had come up smelling so close to the long pier, sheer off so strangely? When she had got to the center of the very nose she was smelling, she seemed suddenly to have lost her sense of smell and to have flanked over to the short pier."

Mr. A. Lincoln suggested a mechanical problem on the boat or that the pilot had not surveyed the conditions around the piers.

The jury listened two days before Lincoln came to a close. He knew that in handling a jury there is a certain moment when it is advantageous to quit talking.

He said, "Gentlemen, I have not exhausted my stock of information, and there are more things I could suggest regarding this case, but as I have doubtless used up my time, I presume I had better close."

The jury was locked up. Their deadlock action was generally taken as a victory for railroads, bridges and Chicago, and against steamboats, river men and Saint Louis.

Newsmen from river towns rushed out of the courtroom to get the news back to their papers. The spectators filed out of the courtroom. There were many sad faces leaving, and some were pleasantly greeting others who had hoped the bridge and the railroad would be the victors.

Among them were Philip, Virginia, and her father. Mr. Lincoln strode up to them, put his arm around Virginia and said,

"I want to thank you for your help in putting together

materials for the trial. It was a great help and gave me an edge."

"You too, Philip. You helped me get familiar with the bridge and the river."

"Mr. Sheffield, your brige is safe now, and you will have made a great step forward in building the great Northwest. War seems inevitable, and the bridge over the Mississippi could become an asset to Northern interests."

"This calls for a celebration," Virginia's father announced.

They decided to take the train back to Rock Island. Virginia's father had access to a private car, but they all decided to go to the parlor car to be with other people who had been in Chicago for the trial.
There was much hand shaking and hugs and the bridge backers congratulated each other. They felt the Judge's decision was a victory for them and the country. Now there was nothing standing in the way of bridges' appearing up and down the Mississippi River and other rivers, for that matter.

Philip and Virginia sat together at the far end of the railroad car. Virginia took Philip's hand, looked him straight in the eye and said,

"How about when we get back we go up to LeClaire and do a rapids trip. I'm ready for it. How about you?"

Philip's eyes lit up,

"Yes, that sounds like a really good idea, Virginia. I had a wire from Captain Brickle saying he was on his way up river from Memphis and needs a pilot through the rapids. We could catch a ride to LeClaire with him."

While everyone talked, Abe Lincoln sat by himself reviewing papers that he had not been able to get to while in court. He was preparing himself for a debate with the well established Democratic Senator Douglas. He would challenge Douglas for the Illinois seat in the U.S. Senate within a year. And as the rest as they say is history.

GLOSSARY

abaft: toward or at the stern: AFT
abeam: on a line at right angles to a ships keel
aboard: on onto, or within a ship
abolition: The act of abolishing: the abolishing of slavery
adrift: without power and without anchor or mooring
afloat: borne on or as if on water
aft: rearward
aground: on or onto the shore or the bottom of a body of water
ahead: in a forward direction or position
along side: side by side with
alongshore: along the shore of a body of water
amidships: in or toward the part of a ship midway between the bow and the stern
anchor: a device used to hold a vessel in a particular place
aport: on or toward the left side of a ship
apron: the area along a waterfront edge of a pier or wharf
arsenal: an establishment for the manufacture or storage of military goods
backwater: water turned back in its course by an obstruction or opposing current
bail: a container used to remove water from a boat
bank: the rising ground above a river or lake
bell: a hollow metalic device that vibrates and gives forth a ringing sound when struck
berth: a place where a ship lies when at anchor or at a wharf
bilge the part of the underwater body of a ship
bulkhead: an upright partition separating compartments
blocks: wooden block through which rope passes giving leverage
buoy: markers in a channel indicating passage
cabin class: a class of accommodations on a passenger ship
capstan: a machine for moving or raising heavy weight by winding cable around a vertical spindle mounted drum that is rotated manually or steam driven

captain: an officer in charge of a ship
careen: to cause a boat to lean over to one side
cleat: to secure to with a rope or boat line
course: the act or action of moving in a prescribed direction
craft: a small boat
current: the swiftest part of a stream or river
deck: a platform in a ship serving as a structural element and forming the floor for its compartments
depth: a deep place in a body of water
diving bell: a diving apparatus consisting of a container or helmet with an air hose from which air is supplied to the diver
dock: a wharf or platform for the loading or unloading of materials
downstream: the natural flow of a stream
draft: load or load pulling capacity
drift: the flow or the velocity of the current of a river
eddy: a current of water or air running contrary to the main current
embankment: a raised structure to hold back water or to carry a roadway
fiery: consisting of fire
fire: a destructive burning
flagstaff: a pole on which to raise a flag
flammable: capable of being easily ignited and of burning with extreme rapidity
flatboat: a flat bottomed boat with square ends
float: buoyed on or in a fluid
galley: the kitchen and cooking space on a ship
gang plank: a movable bridge used in boarding or leaving a boat at a pier
grapnel: small anchor with four flukes or claws used in dragging or grappling operations
gravy: a sauce made from the thickened and seasoned juice of cooked meat
gunwale: a part of a ship where topsides and deck meet
halyard: a rope or tackle for raising or lowering
harbor: a place of shelter or refuge

hatch: a door or opening on a ship's deck
headwater: the source of a stream
heel: to tilt to one a side
hoist: to raise into position by means of tackle
hold: the interior of a ship below decks
inboard: toward the center of ship
instrument: a means whereby something is achieved, performed or furthered
island: a tract of land surrounded by water
keel: a longitudinal timber or plate extending along the center of a boat and often extruding from the bottom
knot: to tie in or with a knot. A unit of measure to determine a ships speed
ladder: a structure used for climbing up or down
lamp: a vessle with a wick for burning oil or other inflamable liquid to produce artificial light
landmark: a mark for designating the boundary of land
lanyard: a piece of rope or line for fastening something in ships
lawyer: one whose profession is to conduct lawsuits for clients or to advise as to legal rights and obligations in other matters
life belt: a life preserver in the form of a buoyed belt
life buoy: a float consisting of a ring of buoyant material to support a person who has fallen into the water
line: a rope, string, cord
lounge car: a railroad passenger car with seats for lounging and facilities for serving refreshments
lurch: a sudden roll of a ship to one side
mainstream: a prevailing current or direction
mark: a unit of measure
marlin spike: a tool used to separate strands of rope
marsh: a tract of soft wet land
moderate breeze: wind having a speed of 13 to 18 miles per hour
mooring: an act of making fast a boat with lines or anchors
Mormon: a church member of the Jesus Christ of Later Day Saints

nautical mile: any of various units of distance used for sea navigation
navigate: to travel by water
oarlock: a u-shaped device for holding an oar in place
outpost: an outlying or frontier settlement
overland: by, upon or across land
packet: a passenger boat carrying mail and cargo on a regular schedule
paddle wheel: a wheel with paddles or boards around its circumference used to propel a boat
personal effects: possessions having a close relationship to one's person
plaintiff: one who commences a personal action or lawsuit to obtain a remedy for an injury to his rights
pontoon: a flatbottomed boat or portable float
poop deck: a partial deck above a ship's main after deck
port: the left side of a ship
promenade deck: an upper deck or an area of a passenger ship where passengers promenade
prosecutor: a person who institutes an official prosecution before a court
punk: wood so decayed as to be dry, crumbly and useful for tinder useful for lighting fuses or explosives
put about: to change the direction of a ship
raft: a collection of logs or timber fastened together for conveyance by water
railroad: to transport by rail, a permanent roadway having two lines of rails attached to ties over which rolling stock is drawn by locomotives propelled by steam power
rearward: toward the back of the ship
right: starboard side of a ship
right-of-way: the right of traffic to take precedence
rip current: a strong surface current flowing outward from shore
ripple: a shallow stretch of rough water in a stream
rise: a movement upward
rising: approaching a stated age
river: a natural stream of water of considerable volume

riverboat: a boat for use on a river
road bed: the bed on which the ties, rails, and ballast of a railroad rest
rudder: a flat piece of wood or metal attached upright to a ship's stern so that it can be turned, causing the ship's head to turn in the same direction
rudder post: an additional sternpost in a single screw ship to which the rudder is attached
sailor: a member of the ship's crew
scuttle: to sink on purpose or by accident
seamanship: the art and skill of handling, working or navigating a ship
semaphore: a visible system of visual signaling by two flags held one in each hand
shallow: a place or area in a body of water
ship mate: a fellow sailor
shipwreck: whena ship has been destroyed, sunk or lost
sink: to become submerged
skipper: the master of a ship
slavery: the practice of slaveholding
slave state: a state in the U.S. in which Negro slavery was legal until the Civil War
slough: a place of deep mud or mire
stack: a vertical pipe above the top deck to carry off smoke
stage coach: a horse-drawn passenger or mail carriage
steamboat: a boat propelled by steam power
steer: to direct the course of a ship
steering gear: a mechanism by which something is steered
stern wheeler: a paddle wheel steamer having a stern wheel instead of side wheels
still water: a part of a stream where the gradient is so gentle there is no visible current
suction pump: a common pump in which water or air is pushed by atmosphere pressure into a partial vacuum under a retreating valved piston on the upstroke and reflux is preventedm by a check valve in the pipe
surge: to rise and fall actively

telegram: a telegraphic dispatch
Tensiometer: an instrument for measuring the surface conditions of liquids
ticker tape: the paper ribbon on which a telegraphic ticker prints off its information
tie-up: a mooring place for boats
trader: a person whose business is buying, selling or bartering
trading post: a station of a trader or trading company established in a sparcely settled region where trade in products of local origin (as furs) is carried on
train: a connected line of railroad cars with or without a steam engine
Uncle Tom: a pious and faithful elderly Negro slave in the novel *Uncle Tom's Cabin* by Harriet Beecher Stone
veteran: an old soldier of long service
walk way: a passage for walking
waterway: a navigable body of water
wheel: to turn on or as if on axis
wheel house: pilothouse
white water: a frothy water (as in breakers, rapids, or waterfalls)
witness: one that gives testimony
wreck: the action of wreaking or fact or state of being wreaked or destroyed
yoke: a crosspiece on the head of a boat's rudder

The author with one of his sculptures that over look the Mississippi.

ABOUT THE AUTHOR

Ted McElhiney is no stranger to the Mississippi River. His father was born and raised on the Father of all Waters at Pontoosuc, Illinois, a sleepy little village which had, as its main industry commercial fishing and hunting. Ted's father, grandfather, and uncle, when not fishing during winter months, would guide wealthy Chicago businessmen onto spotted islands in the Mississippi for goose and duck hunting.

The area where his father grew up was only a few miles from Nauvoo, Illinois and the area where the "Banditti" terrorized the inhabitants for many years in the early 1800's.

Later, in the 1950s, Ted's parents built a second home on a bluff overlooking the Mississippi River at New Boston, Illinois, only a few miles from Muscatine, Iowa. Many weekends were spent there learning about the river and history from his father.

After being discharged from a tour in the United States Navy, Ted attended the University of Illinois studying communications and advertising art. He spent many years as a commercial artist, art director, and creative director for many eastern and Chicago advertising agencies.

He later returned to the Midwest and settled in the Quad-Cities and again back to the banks of the Mississippi River.

Wanting to be in business for himself he formed an advertising agency and commercial art studio. The agency was sold to a popular food franchise, after 28 years of successful operation .

He enrolled in a graduate sculpture program at the University of Iowa to pursue a life long interest in creating sculpture.

Today, he and his wife, Janet, live in a home with a large studio overlooking the Mississippi River at LeClaire, Iowa.

He spends his time creating sculptures of wildlife, people and children. His work can be found across the United States in private collections, parks and commercial businesses.

He and his wife spend much of their leisure time on the river in their cruiser.

His research for this book has been a challenge for many years. It has taken at least five years to completion.

Although many happenings and some characters in this book are fictitious, it is meant to bring a story of the history, not always familiar to all, about what happened here at this place, when working steamboats were prominent. Enjoy a new look at the history of the river during the middle 1800's.

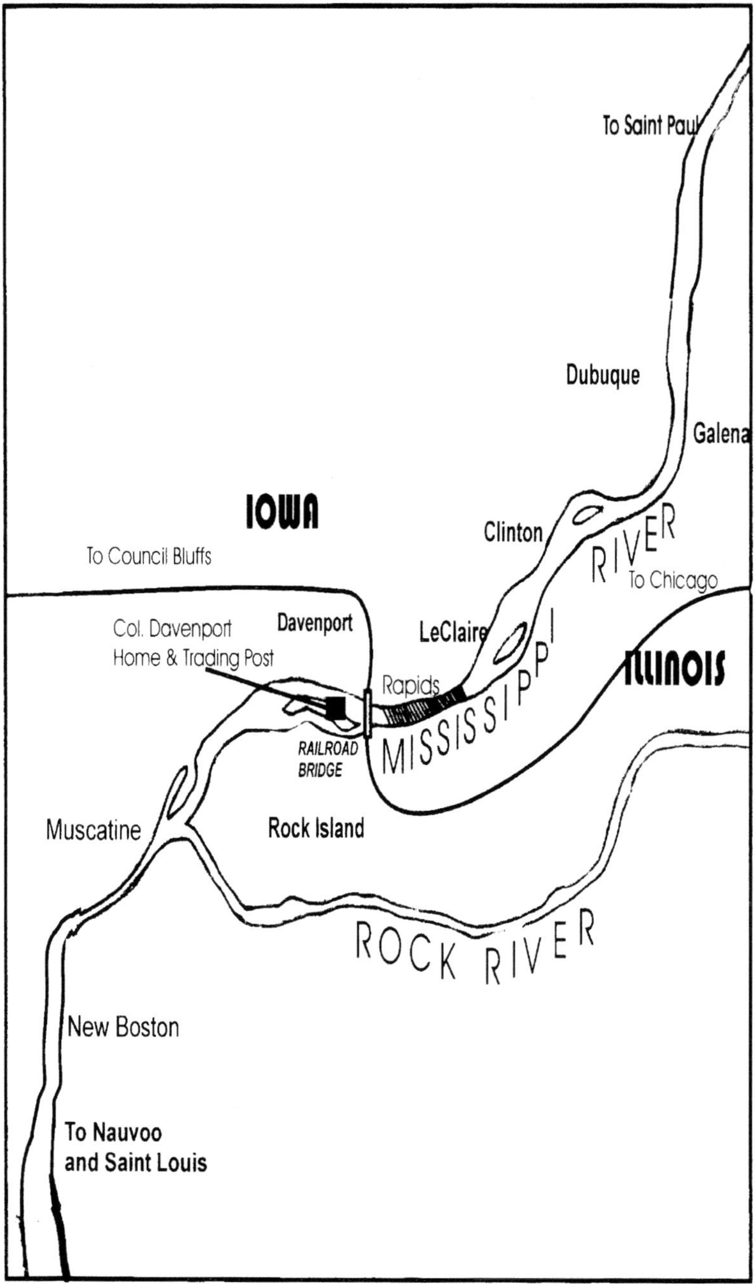
To Saint Paul
Dubuque
Galena
IOWA
Clinton
RIVER
To Council Bluffs
To Chicago
Col. Davenport
Home & Trading Post
Davenport
LeClaire
ILLINOIS
Rapids
MISSISSIPPI
RAILROAD
BRIDGE
Muscatine
Rock Island
ROCK RIVER
New Boston
To Nauvoo
and Saint Louis